OTHERS OF
MY KIND

OTHERS OF MY KIND

A Novel

JAMES SALLIS

B L O O M S B U R Y
NEW YORK · LONDON · NEW DELHI · SYDNEY

Published by Bloomsbury USA, New York

All papers used by Bloomsbury USA are natural, recyclable products made
from wood grown in well-managed forests. The manufacturing processes
conform to the environmental regulations of the country of origin.

LIBRARY OF CONGRESS CATALOGING-IN-PUBLICATION DATA

Sallis, James, 1944–
Others of my kind : a novel / by James Sallis.—First U.S. edition.
pages cm
ISBN: 978-1-62040-209-2 (alk. paper)
1. Kidnapping—Fiction.   2. Girls—Crimes against—Fiction.
3. Post-traumatic stress disorder in adolescence—Fiction.
4. Rehabilitation counseling—Fiction.   I. Title.
PS3569.A462O84 2013
813'.54—dc23
2013012215

First U.S. edition 2013

1 3 5 7 9 10 8 6 4 2

Typeset by Westchester Book Group
Printed and bound in the U.S.A. by Thomson-Shore Inc., Dexter, Michigan

To the memory of my mother,
who knew about secrets
and hard lives

1

AS I TURNED into my apartment complex, sack of Chinese takeout from Hong Kong Garden in hand, Szechuan bean curd, Buddhist Delight, a man stood from where he'd been sitting on the low wall by the bank of flowers and ground out his cigarette underfoot. He wore a cheap navy-blue suit that nonetheless fit him perfectly, gray cotton shirt, maroon tie, oxblood loafers. He had the most beautiful eyes I've ever seen.

"Ms. Rowan? Jack Collins, violent crimes." With an easy, practiced motion he flipped open its wallet to display a badge. "You give me a minute of your time?"

"Why not. Come on up."

Without asking, I spooned food out onto two plates and handed one to him. For a moment he looked surprised, but only for a moment, then tucked in.

"So what can I do for you, Jack Collins?" I asked between bites. We stood around the kitchen island. Tiles chipped at the edge, grout stained by untold years of spills and seasoned by time to a light brown. The kitchen radio, as always, was on. After six the station switches from classical to jazz. Lots of tenor sax. California bebop beating its breast.

"Well, first, I guess, you could tell me why you handed me this plate."

"You're not wearing a wedding ring. Your shirt needs pressing, and even with that suit and tie, you have on white socks. A wife or girlfriend would have called you on that. So I figure you live alone. People who live alone are usually up for a meal. Especially at six thirty of an evening."

"And here I thought *I* was the detective." He forked in the last few mouthfuls of food. "Vegetarian?"

I admitted to it as he went to the sink, rinsed out utensils and plate, and set them in the rack.

"I know what happened to you," he said.

"You mean how I spent my early years."

"Danny and all the rest, yes."

"Those records were sealed by the court."

"Yeah, well . . ."

He came back to collect my dishes and utensils, took them to the sink and rinsed them, added them to the rack. Stood there looking out the window above the sink. Another tell that he's a bachelor, used to living alone. Maybe just a little compulsive.

"Look, I'm just gonna say this. I spent the last few hours up at the county hospital. Young woman by the name of Cheryl got brought in there last night. Twenty years old going on twelve. Way it came about was, the neighbors got a new dog that wouldn't stop barking. They didn't have a clue, tried everything. Then, first chance the dog had, it shot out the door, parked itself outside the adjoining apartment and wouldn't be drawn away. Finally they called nine-one-one. Couple of officers responded, got no answer at the door, had the super key them in. Found Cheryl in a closet, bound and gagged, clothespins on her nipples, handmade dildos taped in place in her vagina and rectum. Guy was a woodworker, apparently—one of the responding officers is a hobbyist himself, says this mook used only the best-quality wood, tooled it down to a high shine. Cheryl didn't talk much to begin with. Then about five this morning she stopped talking at all. Just started staring at us. Like she was behind thick glass looking out."

"Yeah, that's what happens. You get tired of all the questions, you know they're never going to understand."

"Mook got home from work not long after the officers arrived on the scene. Had some sort of club there by the door, apparently, and came at them with it. Junior officer shot him dead, a single shot to the head. Training officer, twenty-plus years on the job, he'd never once drawn his piece."

Collins opened the refrigerator door and rummaged about, extracting a half-liter bottle of sparkling water. Mostly flat when he shook it, but hey. He poured glasses for both of us and threw in sliced limes from the produce drawer.

"Look, you don't want to go back into all that, I'll understand. But we've got nothing but blind alleys north south east and west. No idea who this girl—this woman—is. Where she's from, how long she's been there."

"Twenty going on twelve, you said."

"Could just be shock. One of the doctors mentioned sensory deprivation, talked about developmental lag. A nurse thought she might be retarded. At any rate—" He put a business card on the island between us. "They're keeping her at the hospital overnight, for observation. You see your way clear to visiting her, talking with her, I'd appreciate it."

"I don't think so."

"Fair enough."

"Anyone ever tell you you have beautiful eyes, Officer Collins?"

"My mother used to say that. Funny. I'd forgotten. . . ." He smiled. "Thanks for the meal, Ms. Rowan—and for your time. If by some chance you should happen to change your mind, give me a call, I'll drive."

I saw him to the door, tried to listen to music, picked up a Joseph Torra novel and put it back down after reading the same paragraph half a dozen times, found myself in a bath at two A.M. wide awake and thinking of things best left behind. Not long after six, I was on the phone.

"Hope I didn't wake you."

"No problem. Alarm'll be going off soon anyway."

"Your offer still open?"

Nowadays whenever anyone asks me where I'm from, I tell them Westwood Mall. I love seeing the puzzled look on their faces. Then they laugh.

Everyone here's from somewhere else, so it's doubly a joke.

But I really am from Westwood Mall. That's where I grew up.

I was eight years old when I was taken. I'd had my birthday party the week before, and was wearing the blue sweater my parents gave me, that and the pink jeans I loved, and my first pair of earrings.

His name was Danny. I thought he was old, of course, everybody over four feet tall looked old to me, but he was probably only in his twenties or thirties. He liked Heath bars and his breath often smelled of them. He wasn't much for brushing teeth or bathing. His underarms smelled musty and animal-like, his privates had an acid smell to them, like metal in your mouth. Some days I can still taste that.

I really don't remember much about the first year. Danny kept me in a box under his bed. He'd built it himself. I loved the smell of the fresh pine. He took the jeans and sweater but let me keep my earrings. He'd come home and slide me out, pop the top—two heavy hasps, I remember, two huge padlocks like in photos of Houdini—his own personal sardine. He'd bring me butter pecan sundaes that were always half melted by the time he got home. I felt safe there in the box, sometimes imagined myself as a kind of genie, summoned into the world to grant my summoner's wishes, to perform magic.

I'm not sure I was much more than a doll for him. Something he took out to play with. But he'd be so eager when he came home, so I don't know. His penis would harden the moment I touched it. Sometimes he'd come then, and afterward we'd just lie together on his bed. Other times he'd put things up me, cucumbers, shot glasses, bottles, either up my behind or what he called my cooze. He'd always pet my hair and moan quietly to me when he did that.

He worked as a nurse's aide at DC General and as a corrections officer at the prison, pool and swing shifts at both, irregular hours, so I never had much idea what time of day it was when I felt my box being pulled out. Sometimes, from inside, I'd smell the heavy sweetness of the sundae. I was always excited.

Two years after I was taken, we went to Westwood Mall, the first outing we'd ever had. It was our second anniversary, Danny explained, and he wanted to do something special to celebrate. He gave me a pearl necklace, real pearls, he said, and I promised to behave. He'd even bought a pretty blue dress and shoes for me. At Acropolis Greek I stabbed his hand with a plastic knife, kicked off the shoes, and fled. I was surprised at how easily the knife went in, at the way it broke off when I twisted. Flesh should not be that vulnerable, that penetrable.

After that, I lived in the mall. Found safe places to hide from security guards, came out at night or during the rush hours to dine off an abundance of leftover fast food, had my pick of T-shirts, jackets, and all manner of clothing left behind, read abandoned books and newspapers. I had turned from genie to Ms. Tarzan. Periodically I'd watch from various vantage points as Danny prowled the mall hoping to find me. You may remember apocryphal tales of Mall Girl, sightings of which were first reported at Westwood then quickly spread throughout the city's other malls. Eventually everyone came to believe the whole thing was ex nihilo, spun from vapor to whole cloth, no more than a self-serving stunt. The journalist who first reported these tales and devoted weeks of her column to following up on them, Sherry Bayles, was summarily fired. Lack of journalistic integrity, the paper cited. Later, when she was working as a substitute teacher, more or less by simple chance we became friends. She's the only one I ever told about my days in the mall. Endearingly, she did no more than smile and nod.

My Edenic time at Westwood ended after eighteen months. A newly hired security guard believed the stories and lay in wait for me long after his shift was done. I was biting into half a leftover hamburger I'd fished out of one of the trash containers when he came up behind me and said, "I'd be happy to buy you a whole one." His name was Kevin, a really nice man. He bought me that hamburger, complete with fries and shake, on the way to the police station. There a Mrs. Cabot from Family Services picked me up.

So the second—third? fourth?—act of my life began.

Next morning I woke up in what they call a holding facility. Whatever they called it, it was an animal pen, thirty or forty kids all stuffed in there. One of them came snuffling around my bed like a pig after truffles around three A.M. and left with a bloody nose, down one tooth. At eight they gave me a breakfast of underdone, runny eggs with greasy bacon mixed in and carted me off to see a social worker.

She said her name was Miss Taylor. "The report states that you've been living on your own in the mall. Is that right?"

"Yes, ma'am."

"And you're eleven?"

"Almost twelve."

"You told the admitting nurse that before this, you spent two years in a box under someone's bed."

Miss Taylor was sitting behind a desk in an office chair. She rocked back and forth, staring at me. When she rocked back, she went out of sight. There she was. Gone. There she was again.

"The nurse thinks you made that up."

"I don't make things up."

"You also said that during that time he repeatedly abused you."

"That's not what I said."

Ignoring me, she went on: "That he touched you in inappropriate places, put his member in you."

"His penis, you mean."

"Yes. His penis."

"Sometimes he did. More often it was other stuff."

I'd made her out to be just another office zombie, but now she looked up, and her eyes brimmed with concern. You never know when or where these doors will open.

"Poor thing," she said. "I'm so sorry."

"Why?"

"Sweetheart—"

"My name's Jenny."

"Jenny, then. Adults are supposed to care for children, not take advantage of them."

"Danny did take care of me. He brought me sundaes. He fed me, he cleaned my box. Took me out when he came home."

Tears replaced the concern brimming in her eyes. I had the feeling that habitually they waited back there a long time; and that when they came, they pushed themselves out against her will.

She tried to cover by ducking her head to scribble notes.

Three days later Mrs. Cabot showed up again to escort me to what everyone kept calling "a juvenile facility," half hospital, half prison. (Daily my vocabulary was being enriched.) The buildings were uniformly ugly, all of them unrelievedly rectangular, painted dull gray and set with double-glass windows that made me think of fish tanks. I was assigned a narrow bed and lockless locker in Residence A—a closed ward, the attendant explained. Everyone started out here, she said, but if all went well, soon enough I'd be transferred to an open ward.

That was the extent of my orientation. The rest I got onto by watching and following along. Each morning at six we had ten minutes to shower. Then the water was turned off, though there weren't enough showerheads to go around and even when we doubled up, some girls were left waiting. After that we had ten minutes to use toilets in open stalls before being marched in a line through a maze of covered crosswalks to the dining room. Captives from other residences, boys and girls alike, would just be finishing their breakfasts. We waited outside like ants at a picnic. Once the occupying forces were mustered on the crosswalk opposite, we entered.

School was next, three or four grades and easily twice as many ages lumped into one, with a desperate teacher surfing from desk to desk looking as though this, staying in motion, might be all that kept her from going under. Each hour or so an attendant materialized to cart a roll-call group of us away for group therapy (equal parts self-dramatization, kowtowing by inmates, and surreptitious psychological bullying by therapists), occupational therapy (same old plastic lanyards, decoupage, and ashtrays), weekly one-on-ones with the facility's sole psychiatrist (a sad man whose hopelessly asymmetrical shoulders accepted without protest the dandruff falling like silent, secret snow upon them). Occasionally one of our troop would be led off for shock therapy only to return with eyes glazed, mother's milk of her synapses curdled to cheese rind, unable to recognize any of us, to recall where she was or remember to get out of bed to pee or, if she did, to locate the bathroom. One or another of us would take her by the hand and lead her, help her clean up afterward.

I could provide little useful information about my parents or my origin. Scoop the fish from the bowl, which is the whole of what the fish knows, how can the fish possibly describe it to you? Family Services's own searches came to naught as well. Back then few enough possibilities for tracking existed. Children's fingerprints went unrecorded. Enforcement, legal, and support services were not so much islands as archipelagoes. I'd been taken more or less at random and kept, first by Danny, then by myself, in seclusion. Four years had passed. Essentially I *had* no identity.

The long and short of it was, I got assigned as a ward of the court and, barring foster placement, which we all knew to be about as likely as universal health care during a Republican administration, was remanded by the court to the juvenile facility "until such time as the aforesaid attains her majority." This majority, I found as I burrowed into outdated law books for impenetrable reasons ensconced in the facility's woeful library, was not fixed. I could petition for same after my sixteenth birthday.

In addition, the court's ruling decreed twice-yearly reviews by the board. For the first couple of reviews I showed up and said my piece, watching women in sober dresses and men in short-sleeved white shirts nod their heads, claiming they understood. Sure they did. As they went home to their families, Barcaloungers, TVs, chicken-and-mashed-potato dinners. I could see why it was called a board. No bending here, just sheer functionality. Nothing came of those first command performances, of course, and after that I stopped caring. Until age sixteen, when indeed I did petition the court—not the mental-health, juvenile courts to which I'd been restricted the last few years but an adult, open court. I'd spent considerable time in the facility's library researching this, doing my best to get my ducks all in a row, even if some quackery were involved.

Mall security guard Kevin, onetime journalist Sherry Bayles, Family Services agent Mrs. Cabot, and social worker Miss Taylor were all there to testify on my behalf. Appropriately demure and deferential, I walked out emancipated. Miss Taylor set up residence for me in a halfway house. "Just until you get on your feet," she assured me.

It was an upscale part of town where, whenever you emerged blinking into sunlight, homeowners on adjacent porches and in neighboring fenced yards stared at you as though you might be a cabbage that had somehow managed to uproot itself and learn to walk. (God knows how the property came to this purpose. Some old-money donation, possibly trying to memorialize an addicted wife or child?) I always smiled my biggest smile, said good morning with eyes steady on these neighbors, and inquired how they were doing on this fine day. By the third week they were calling me over to ask how it was going.

Not spectacularly well, as it happened. Once prospective

employers heard I was sixteen, had spent four years in a state facility, and had never before worked, the interview was pretty much over. Never mind court papers certifying me as an adult, or my own composure and comportment at these interviews. Two months in, I began having the terrible feeling that halfway might be as far as I was going to get. I mentioned this when I stopped to chat with old Miss Garrett at the end of the block. She was out in her garden weeding flowers as usual. How those weeds managed to regrow overnight, *every* night, I never understood. But there she was each morning in ancient pink pedal pushers and sky-blue straw hat, pulling those suckers up with her own rootlike, ar-thritic hands.

"If you don't mind swing shifts and long hours, honey, I've got a nephew with his own business who's looking for a waitress. Figure you can handle pushy men?"

Her nephew's diner turned out to be within walking distance, fourteen blocks away at the far edge of the business district. Miss Garrett had called ahead. Not only did Bernard ("Call me Benny") have a job, he had a room above the diner for rent, cheap, if I was interested. Miss Taylor wasn't too happy about that when I called to talk about it, and to tell her I'd got a job. Did I think it a good idea to dump all my eggs in one basket? was the way she put it. But I wanted desperately, after all those years of absolute depen-dence, to be on my own. I could almost taste it, like that drop of sweet dew you pull out of honeysuckle, like the metallic taste of Danny's genitals. And it was after all, as Miss Taylor asserted, my decision to make, and mine only.

That in itself to me was miraculous. Absolutely miraculous. My decision to make.

I worked for Benny for close to five years. Poured thousands of cups of coffee, clipped order after order to the stainless steel carousel that spun around to the kitchen, handled my share of drunk, unruly, unbearable, bearish men, joked and traded insults with short-order cooks who came and went with such frequency that none of us bothered to keep track of their names, after many a workday plodded back down the outside stairway to pull another shift when the waitress du jour or de la nuit didn't show, soaked red, swollen feet as much in abject apology to those poor dependent appendages as for any palliative effect.

It had been a rocky first shift—but then again, I've always been a quick study. And halfway in, I'd nailed it.

"Aunt Mae hasn't failed me yet," Benny told me my first week. "I knew when she sent you my way it would work out. I just never expected it was gonna work out this well."

I was freshly off duty, diner closed for the night. Illegal aliens, I assumed, unregistered workers anyway, would be doing scutwork: scouring the grill, disinfecting toilets, sinks and chop surfaces, dumping grease pans. Benny had asked me to stick around. I was a little nervous about that. Now he disappeared into the kitchen to emerge with slices of apple pie for both of us.

"You charm them all, Jenny. I wish I knew how you do it. Guys who've been coming in here for years, hating everything from our cole slaw to the stools at the counter to the shades on the windows, suddenly they're asking for you, wanting to know what tables you're covering."

"It's good, being liked."

"Yes. It is. Good for business, too."

Rotating with thumb and second finger his coffee cup in its shallow corral of saucer, round and round, he asked me how the pie was. The best, I told him.

If that cup broke out of the circle, if any of us came to question appearances too closely, all havoc might ensue.

Benny smiled.

"Go get yourself some sleep, girl. We're here."

And so he was. Squarely behind me when I put in hours for my GED and needed time off to study, when I took the test and passed, when I signed up for community college and found myself fifty dollars and change short of fees. Benny countersigned the loan on my first car, a Buick Regal resembling nothing so much as a shell used up and moved out of.

We is another matter. Benny was on his third wife then. The first had skipped with no forwarding address, taking with her the only child Benny was ever to have. The second was diagnosed with MS early in their marriage; Benny spent the next ten years caring for her. Number three flitted about town in a red Mercedes convertible Benny could ill afford, touching down periodically in pressed jeans and clear plastic heels.

It took me two semesters, not four, to complete requirements for the associate degree. Always a quick study, as I said. I was still working better than full-time then, seven or eight shifts a week. When I hauled a right turn to the state college nearby, Benny did what he could to work around my schedule, and I reciprocated by filling in the blanks in his whenever possible. One holiday weekend I remember working something like thirty-six hours straight. Patrons' faces became elastic blobs like those in lava lamps. Walls warped toward me as I approached. I would come to and find myself staring into coffee cups or into the folds of the napkins of setups, wondering how long I'd been standing there and what messages I'd imagined these things might have for me.

Even after moving to the new job, I stayed on at Benny's apartment, which felt like the only home I'd had.

It was there, on a warm Friday in April, that I brought Michael, my first guest in all those years. We worked together in postproduction at the local television station, WAAT, affectionately referred to as WHAT by its watchers, where I'd been much taken with Michael's quick laugh and Old South manners as he compulsively opened doors for women, stood when elders entered the room, tacked *sir* or *ma'am* (or so it seemed) onto every sentence. He was a few years younger than me, many more years a member of the proper world. Both of us were prodigies of a sort, another thing that brought us together.

I'd always thought of the scars as something I *put on*, like clothes or a hat, not part of me at all, nothing to do with my essential self. Michael, bless him, never once gave any indication that he'd so much as noticed them. He lay beside me as though all this were the most natural thing in the world.

Moths hit the window and skittered down it.

"You're not disappointed?" I asked.

What I meant was, repulsed.

"Why on earth would I be?"

My head fit so well into the hollow of his shoulder. His hand lay lightly along my ribs. Moonlight in passing peered through my window, leaving its imprint or memory behind, a luminous door there by the bed, minutes before it moved on to other windows, other lives.

2

BACK TO PRESENT TIME—past present, I should say. Eight-fourteen on a warm morning in May, when I first began jotting down notes for this in an old accounting ledger. I'm sitting in a red-and-white kitchen drinking green tea under a blue sky listening to news on the radio. Leaves of trees outside my window scarcely moving. High wind and possible thunderstorms later in the day, the radio cautions. Neighbors shower, water lawns, walk dogs, cart recycle bins to curbside, back SUVs out of driveways to let passenger cars exit.

From my spider-colonized patio I watched dawn nose its way back into the world. Light sketched out the form of trees before filling them in. Candy pink of bougainvillea, impossible white of oleander ever more vivid. Then suddenly—though I'd followed its approach for most of an hour—morning.

Cherishing night's enclosure, I tend to sleep little.

From the radio I gathered that we were engaged in another war about which I hadn't heard heretofore. Words such as *liberation*, *democracy* and *freedom* blazed up like fireflies from commentary and call-ins, with that same cold, momentary light. Once upon a time there was a pretense that such wars had to be declared. Apparently no longer.

Meanwhile, just before dawn that morning (as I sat on my patio watching daylight patch itself together), another plane lowered toward the White House and was shot down. This was getting to be a regular thing. As many as eighty dead, untold injured, fires still burning. President Burke had been spirited away. Onto a continuously flying Air Force One? To the sanctuary of some war room? Vice President Courtney-Phillips was likewise unavailable, tucked away elsewhere behind a thicket of Secret Service agents.

Radio had been a constant companion since Michael gave me my first, saying "You shouldn't be so alone." Never mind that I like being alone. Never mind that I work in TV where day after day I take up fragments—tape, voice-overs, audio notes—and shape them into a simulacrum of the real world. I'd never have suspected I could have any taste for further such decantings. But radio's subtle voices won me over, became the sound track of my life. They were there—simply muted—as I worked, shopped for groceries, sat in the mall over coffee watching people of every sort come and go.

Observing, I suppose, would be the more accurate verb.

Lacking any semblance of childhood, having spent my adolescence in the wild as it were, I could fit in only by a kind of adaptation scarcely known outside the insect world. I mimicked those about me, finally with such vigor that few were able to distinguish conjured image from real. Even I sometimes confused the two.

Time now to rouse myself, shower, find clothes. This is what people do. At the studio, in fragments of tape and film, a shattered world waited to be put back together again.

There's something happening here, the bathroom radio, set to an oldies station, intoned. *What it is ain't exactly clear.*

This is what I remember about my mother: she deplored silence. Radios and TVs inhabited every room, bathroom and kitchen included. At table there had to be conversation, and in the kitchen afterward as well, as she did dishes, put up leftovers, and obsessively swabbed the stove. She filled any vacant spaces, any ellipses, with grunts of appreciation for the food, throat clearings, hummed snatches of unidentifiable songs. That's *all* I remember of her.

Drawing the shower curtain closed, I felt safe in a way I never will outside. Just as I go back to the mall at every opportunity, an immigrant returning to the homeland, and feel safe there. What no one understands is that, lying there in the box under Danny's bed, miraculously I was able to stop being myself and to become so much more. I could feel myself liquefying, flowing out into the world. I became numinous. Sometimes, though ever less often as time goes by, I'm able to recapture that.

Black jeans, pink T-shirt chopped off at midriff level, half-heels. Gray blazer over. Warrior dress.

"I called in saying I'd be late, but shouldn't take too long."

"So I guess breakfast is out."

"How about dinner instead—if you're free?"

"You're on."

Jack Collins's ride was an early-eighties Buick custom-painted and slightly raked, and you could tell he was self-conscious to be driving this young man's car, which he'd had since he was seventeen. Not much else in his life had proven that enduring or dependable, he said. Bought it with what he'd earned working construction the summer he graduated from high school.

Cheryl was everything I expected, a plain girl like myself, quiet and superficially ingratiating, with still eyes that reminded me of my onetime friend Bishop, or of walls spackled with unreadable graffiti.

Collins took me in and introduced me, then discreetly withdrew.

What can I say? I told her how I had come to pass the middle years of my admittedly short life, and at what cost. I talked about not carrying forward regrets, about simply getting on with things. Halfway through, it occurred to me that what I was saying sounded not at all different from the harangues that hundreds of teenagers suffer daily from parents. We all think we're special, somehow exempt. When the real lesson's how much alike we all are.

I told her I'd check back with her later, that she shouldn't hesitate to call me if she needed to talk, any time, day or night. Wrote my name and number on the back of a deposit slip, the only piece of paper I could find at liberty in my purse.

"Miss Rowan?"

To that point Cheryl had given no indication she was listening, not the least register of recognition, as I spoke.

"Yes?"

"Where are they going to take me next?"

For her, I well knew, the world seemed at this point little more than a congress of *theys*, dozens of *theys* shoving her about like a pawn on the board. Pawns had no say in things, pawns were sacrificed, pawns got captured and went away.

"Some kind of holding center would be my guess. You're over-age for the state juvenile facility. They'll probably try for a shelter of some sort. Depends on what's available. I'll call in later, find out where you are."

Jack Collins held up one hand in abject apology as I walked out and caught him with sacks in the other.

"I had nothing to do with this. They followed me home. I swear. Can we keep them?"

Bagels and coffee.

We ate them sitting in his Buick in the parking lot outside WAAT, not talking much, watching traffic on the elevated turn-around a block away, watching a police chopper hover somewhere near downtown.

"I'm really late," I said, draining my cup. Grace would have another waiting for me inside.

"So am I. Or will be by the time I get there." Finishing off his bagel, licking stray cream cheese from fingers, he set the rest of his coffee in its glazed paper cup in the holder behind the gearbox.

I reached for the door handle only to find his hand lightly on my arm.

"Thank you, Jenny."

"You're welcome."

"How late do you work?"

"Sixish."

"Well, since I've stranded you here, I have to give you a ride home."

"I can take the bus, no problem."

"Sorry. That's the rule."

"Oh my God, there are rules?"

"And besides, we're doing dinner."

Leaning over, I kissed his cheek and told him yes we were, and I looked forward to it. If this were an old-time movie and we'd been standing, I'd probably have gone up on one foot. I said I'd give him a call.

Grace handed off a coffee as I swung past. You'll need to zap it, she said. I know, I know, I told her, *this* late I didn't plan on. I could swear sometimes that Grace has multiple built-in clocks.

She can be working at one of the computers, completely absorbed in her task, then, two minutes before something else needs doing or an appointment comes due, she'll surface. I thanked her for the coffee and asked after her husband, who months back had been diagnosed with cancer. Holding his own, she said. Chemo's working—so far. She'd got used to the sound of retching in the night, and to his prowling the house, unable to sleep.

In my studio the blazer and shoes went off, warrior dress was no more. Everyone called it my office, but there was nothing officelike about it, and here, working, I was utterly alone, absolutely on my own. No one intruded. News- and anchormen, directors, camera jockeys, producers, the occasional intrusive actor—all that got dealt with elsewhere. Here, I lived among frames and clips and soundings, pure abstractions. For that moment in time it came down to date-coded footage of gutted apartment complexes and refugee lines, tapes of reporters-at-the-scene, snippets of talking-head military men and civilian experts. I was focusing so intently that when Michael came to ask if I'd join him for lunch I was startled to realize it had gotten to be one o'clock. Michael and I hadn't been together for years, yet remained close.

"Welcome back to earth," he said.

Always a hard landing.

He glanced at the screen. "Bombing escalated as of this morning. Word just came in that they're offering a bounty on every U.S. serviceman killed."

I begged off lunch, explaining that I'd come in late.

"Delivered to the door personally, it's said, by one of our city's finest."

No one with whom I work knows anything of my past. They wonder, though. Curiosity peeks out from behind pillars of small talk and rodomontade. My lack of history becomes a kind of negative space, a gravity. Worldly things bend and swim and fall toward it.

"A friend," I said.

"Of course. And as for lunch, no problem. But just for that, tomorrow you buy."

By two I had a rough cut for the spot on our latest undeclared war, more than an hour of video and tape boiled down to a broth of just over a full minute, and what easily might have been a full day's work. Depending on available broadcast time, further cuts and assembly would be made by proper news editors, but it was out of my hands now, wrapped and delivered, as good as it was going to get.

I turned then to files of raw footage for a documentary on PO-box schools offering diplomas and degrees on a pay-your-money-take-your-choice basis, running through it all, staying loose and letting it roll, for the moment not thinking about nips or tucks, what I'd take out, what I'd leave in.

What I thought about instead, as those images and voices washed over me, was Bishop back at the halfway house, maybe the first friend I'd ever had. Doctors operating pro bono like lawyers had told him his spleen was shot, kidneys barely functional, liver operating at 10 percent. We can't say it'll help much if you quit doing drugs and alcohol, they told him, but you'll die slower. Immediately he took that as his slogan, showing up with T-shirts for all of us, DIE SLOWER! printed across front and back.

Last time I saw him was in an apartment just off downtown that Miss Taylor found for him. That part of the city had gone to seed pretty much by then; what once was a luxury hotel now hosted transients, enfeebled elderly, exiles from psychiatric hospitals, and long-out-of-work entertainers. In the apparition appearing before me I barely recognized my friend. He'd grown thin and

21

gray, his body clenched around arthritic pain that could be ame-liorated only by the aspirin that, if he took it, opened fissures of blood in his esophagus and stomach. Eyes that once seemed to me to hold the world entire, all the world's marvel, multitudi-nousness and mystery, now were dull stone. He still wore one of his DIE SLOWER! T-shirts, letters faded to illegibility. To my shame, I took the first opportunity and fled. He called a couple of times after that, but I never answered or went back. To my eternal shame.

By four I had a rough cut of the bogus-diploma feature and, delivering it to my producer, asked what else was on the boards.

"*Damn*, girl," Mickie said, eyes slightly out of focus from too many early mornings and too many demands coming down the draw from suits and sharp-creased MBAs above, "I just now got the New Olgate package you kicked upstairs earlier. You trying to make the rest of us look like slackers or what?"

Those suits and MBAs were the very reason she had dropped back to a local station; now it seemed they'd followed her. Going on sixty, with the body and attitude of a thirty-year-old, Mickie'd been around damn near since TV news started. She was as re-sponsible as anyone else for the form and direction it took. She was also the one who hired me.

I'd signed up for an art course, at which I was hopelessly in-ept, taught by a friend of hers who died of AIDS four years later, and from sheer desperation had started doing collage. Come to meet her friend for lunch, Mickie saw a piece of mine—snatches of blurry satellite surveillance photos, the CIA seal juxtaposed with the USDA stamp put on meats, photos of emaciated bodies of children in the Far East placed about the edge of a U.S. gro-cery ad in the manner of medieval illustrations—and took an in-terest. By month's end I had dropped out of college and was working for her, shown the ropes by Luis who (her expression, my sentiment) knew everygoddamnthing.

By six I'd put to good use all she and Luis had taught me and got a solid start on the new project, the profile of a journeyman African-American senator from Maryland who, though he denied it, appeared to be inching toward a run for president. Exciting stuff. Clichés and grand intentions coming down like showers of rain. Mud puddles at your feet.

Jack waved from behind the Buick's windshield as I emerged, then hurried out and around to open the passenger door for me.

"Rough day?"

"Good one, really. You?"

"So-so. Though I guess, in my line of work, so-so's a good day."

He pulled into the parking lot of a bar ten or twelve blocks away, in a long-decayed portion of the city beginning to show signs of afterlife. Windows and a small plaque over the door read FOUNDATION. "This okay with you?" he asked. When I said it was, we went in. Well-appointed floor plan, good tables with plenty of room between them, and clean, but not much of anyone around save those at the bar, day-long drinkers, regulars. I asked for white wine, Jack ordered a beer and shot. The wine was sickly sweet.

"Thanks again for touching base with Cheryl."

"I only hope that eventually it may do some good."

"What we all hope. You never know." He threw back his shot of well bourbon, sipped a couple ounces of draft. Louis Armstrong's "What a Wonderful World" played over a sophisticated sound system. Someone was losing big money here.

"Have to tell you this one thing," Jack said.

"Okay . . ."

"I have an ex-wife—not really *ex*, I guess, since all we are is separated. Divorce's been in the works awhile. We have a daughter."

I waited.

"Just wondered how you felt about it," he said, "that's all."

Background music shifted to Israel Kamakawiwo'ole's ukulele-and-solo-voice rendition of "Somewhere Over the Rainbow/What a Wonderful World."

"What's your daughter's name?"

"Deanna."

"You love her?"

"Oh yes."

"See her often?"

"I used to, when she was young. Had her for weekends, half the summer. As she grew up, I saw her less and less."

"Just how long has this divorce been in the works?"

"Little over ten years."

"You check with Ripley, see if that's some kind of record?"

"Think I should?"

"Probably."

His eyes were bright with good humor.

"We all have to decide what's important to us and fight for it, Jack. Sometimes the best way to fight is to do nothing."

"Friends I have left say I'm living in the past, trying to hold on to something that's no longer there."

"The past is what we are, even as we're constantly leaving it."

"You know what? I have no idea what that means."

"Neither do I," I said, laughing. "But it sounded good."

"Let's get some food. There's a mom-and-pop place around the corner. Best Italian in town, everything handmade, even the pasta."

"That sounds good, too."

"What's important to you?" Jack asked as we walked out.

Night was settling in, last tatters of daylight become pink banners riding low in the sky. When he took my arm to gently guide me left, our eyes met.

"Everything," I told him.

Man, this frail biped, moves onto African plains dominated by large animals, hopelessly overpowered. But he has in his hands tools never before seen in the world—clubs, sharpened rocks; later, spears—and in his heart a fierceness those other animals will never embrace, never understand.

I woke from a too-familiar dream, in which I'd been chased by some unknown animal into a blind alley and there among trash bins, naked, had turned to face it with my hatchet of chipped flint bound with vines onto split bamboo, to learn via morning radio that the president has returned to residence in the White House. First Lady Fiona and daughter Fina remain tucked away somewhere in the country's folds. Vice President Courtney-Phillips also hovers out of sight. Further threats have been made, the White House press secretary states. Our intelligence gives these threats credence. We will keep you informed.

Of course they will. Just as they rushed to inform us of actual body counts in Vietnam, U.S.-engineered assassinations in Chile, the systematic closing down of power plants before the energy crisis of 2002, the cost of the Iraq War, or how deregulation might lead to financial collapse.

Firmly seated at the front of the bus, so utterly accustomed to privilege that its presence has become invisible to them, our horde of senators, congressmen, secretaries-of, advisers, attorneys, and lobbyists goes on deciding what is best for us. Little wonder that we feel helpless—ridden. The bureaucracy protects itself;

that becomes its purpose. The machine has no off switch. As Bishop used to say: We're set on SPIN, forever.

Last night's meal had been wondrous. Mr. Bevelaque ("Everyone calls me Papa") hummed what sounded like "Santa Lucia" as ceremonially he wiped the waxcloth of our table, dealt setups of silverware wrapped in napkins, brought a bottle of Chianti and tall glasses of water.

"Go for the special," Jack said. "Most places, with specials they're just trying to offload overorders or dodgy product. Here, it's what's best."

So we had two specials, salmon and asparagus in cream sauce over penne pasta, preceded by bruschetti of sun-dried tomatoes and pesto. The Chianti was good, fruity, with just enough of a bite to it.

Jack had dropped me off around ten. I'd fallen almost immediately to sleep. Then woke fleeing some unknown beast.

I lay still, the neighborhood so quiet that I heard power lines swinging on their posts in the wind, or thought I could. A subtle music. Then suddenly, prompted by that, came a rare memory. It's late night, Saturday, a storm winding down outside. Power has been out. The radio is on in the kitchen, and my mother is alone in there. I hear her, consistently half a step off, singing along.

3

TWO YEARS AGO, I went looking for my parents on the Internet. I'm still not sure why.

Since I had no identity and few early memories, my official life having in effect begun at age almost-twelve, it proved a difficult task.

I assumed, first, that I had been abducted not too far from my home. The car trip to Westwood Mall when Danny and I traveled there to celebrate our anniversary had lasted no more than thirty, forty minutes. Westwood Mall being just outside Harpers Ferry, I focused my search on Harpers Ferry and the cluster of smaller towns surrounding it.

Birth certificates and the like are matters of public record. Counting back, given that even my age was an assumption and allowing for a couple years' slippage either side, I began with a list of close to eight hundred names.

Other records—newspaper archives, school enrollment, church membership—aren't always easy to access, but with persistence you can flush them out.

Hospital records, missing-persons reports filed with

police—here the real problems start. But if calling from a TV station where you're in preproduction on a documentary about, say, preteen disappearances, or the legend of Mall Girl, or a human-interest piece on grandparents seeking long-lost grandchildren, sometimes you find doors easing open.

As somber autumn gave way to bright winter and that in turn to chattering spring, the list shrank to just over six hundred, then to five and a half, four hundred, two hundred plus. I'd get home from the studio to burn away the rest of my evening on Internet and phone. Week by week, I slogged away and pared it down. I'd look out my window and see leaves gone crimson, cinnamon, purple and orange. Next time I glanced up, birds were alighting with straw, bits of fabric and fast-food wrappers in their beaks, building nests among green leaves.

The local NPR station launched a weekend marathon, forty-eight hours of continuous Irish music, about an eighth of which I managed to tape.

On one of the commercial radio stations, curiously, advertisements for new fall TV shows began appearing.

Another started late-night broadcasting of radio dramas from the forties and fifties.

Sweaters and scarves came out of drawers and went back in.

Women's shoes got uglier.

The first of many gifts Danny gave me was something called a Magic 8-Ball. His father had given him one just like it when he was my age, he said, and after all these years he'd had the devil of a time finding one. "You ask a question," he explained, "then turn it over," demonstrating. A triangular piece like a tiny pyramid floated to the surface within. It read *Better not tell you now.*

In my box beneath the bed I held hard on to that Magic

8-Ball. I couldn't see it there, or lift my arm to manipulate it, but it gave me comfort, it was solid, it *knew* things.

For years afterward I didn't think about the 8-Ball, didn't remember it. Then one day as I worked on a documentary about natural structures in architecture I was watching a clip put together by one of the computer geeks, basically animated sketches of geometric shapes. Lines appeared onscreen, came together slowly turning—and there it was. An icosahedron, I later learned: a polyhedron with twenty faces. The tiny pyramid within the 8-Ball. And with that, it all came back. *Signs point to yes. Reply hazy, try again. Outlook good. Don't count on it.*

For a long time that's how my days were, like that icosahedron floating up out of the surround bearing inscrutable texts. Everything became a blur. I worked, stopped off for takeout on the way home, settled into following up the latest leads or scrambling after new ones, dribbled plum sauce and bits of kung pao vegetables on my keyboard.

"You're obsessing," my friend Kimmie told me.

She had called to get together for lunch and, despite my repeated demurrals, kept calling until I agreed.

Kimmie was Vietnamese. We'd met years back in my first computer class, at the time I was first getting dragged, heels scraping, into the modern world. Kimmie was there because on her own she owned real estate and, with her family, a number of convenience stores and a restaurant, and kept books for all. If it hadn't been for her, I'd never have made it through that class. She was one of the few who knew my history.

"Why do you want this?" she asked. "What are you thinking will happen?"

Embarrassed to have no appropriate response, I shrugged.

I was the eminently practical person who met every challenge headlong, snuffling out problem spots large and small, patching them up or over. And I passed my workdays making sense of the world for others, taking up fragments of sensation and information and piecing them together, stitching quilts from leftovers and rag-ends of the world's fabric.

"The Internet's a godsend to you," Kimmie said, "it's where you feel most comfortable. There, you're able to convince yourself you're connected to the world, when in fact you're protected from it, isolated, alone and safe."

"Still in my box, you mean."

She took my hand on the table.

"Friends can say these things."

We spooned up dumplings, punctured them with chopsticks, and sucked out the broth while all around us there at the mall streamed people whose worlds would never include dinners of insect-riddled, half-rotten rice, helicopters struggling to heave whole families up, up and away out of a ravaged city, or young women living in boxes beneath beds.

Four days after that meal with Kimmie, bells rang.

Mr. and Mrs. Horace Smith. Smith—can you believe it? I suppose that in some unswept corner of my mind I still thought of myself as exceptional, so how could I have come from an ordinary two-bedroom block-construction house on Second Street?

Mr. Smith had recently retired from the factory at which he'd worked all his adult life, sending thousands upon thousands of toasters, coffeemakers, electric can openers, and knife sharpeners down the belt into boxes. Wife Edith was a stay-at-home but did volunteer work for the church. The Smiths' only child, a daughter, had disappeared a quarter century ago.

Casa Smith sat halfway down, on the east side, of a block of others just like it. It was white now, but older coats of blue showed beneath. The yard had been recently cut; hedges remained untrimmed and runners of weed extended up onto sidewalk and driveway. Clean windows were not a priority. A white cat sat in one of them watching as I came up the walk, its eyes as cloudy as the window. Do cats, I wondered, have cataracts?

I'd just stepped onto the porch when the mailman swung by. Without comment or question, seeing me there, he handed me the mail.

I rang, and heard the bell go off inside.

Did I see anything of myself in the woman who moments later swung the door open?

She took the mail from my hand.

"You're not Eddie," she said.

"Eddie?"

"Our regular postman."

The door was already closing.

"Mrs. Smith?"

"Yes?"

She glanced back into the house. Hundreds of things in there that needed attending to, no doubt.

"I called, earlier?"

"Oh. From the television station."

"Yes ma'am."

"And you brought my mail. Well then, come right on in."

The front door opened directly into a living room of pale green stucco walls. A sectional sofa too large by half for the room sat against the right wall, an equally outsize entertainment center against the wall opposite, leaving room for little else but a couple of brittle-looking chairs and gimpy end tables. Beige carpet wall to wall, a veldt. All was spotless, ordered. Above the sofa, at the juncture of ceiling and wall, strands of cobweb swayed. Looking from these to her glasses and the watery eyes behind, I understood that the cobwebs were there only because Mrs. Smith could not see them.

"May I offer you coffee?" she asked, smile brightening. "We've just put on a fresh pot. Most people have coffee *after* the meal, but my husband always likes his before." She smiled and added (pointedly?) "We eat at seven."

"Coffee would be wonderful."

Gone perhaps five minutes, she returned with a tray bearing a coffee carafe, cups and saucers, and reservoirs of sugar and milk, bearing in her wake, as well, Mr. Smith.

"When we spoke on the phone," she said, once Mr. Smith had been deposited in what was obviously his accustomed chair and the coffee distributed, "I couldn't quite understand what it was you wanted. Just what is it we can do for you, dear?"

"You had a daughter, Emily."

"We did, yes."

"In April of 1984 she was abducted."

"So we've always assumed."

"Went missing, anyway," Mr. Smith said. "That's how the police put it. 'She went missing.'"

Mr. Smith glanced longingly at the TV. Dark now—as they say of theaters on off days—but filled with promise. Everything came together there, everything made sense.

Mrs. Smith poured more coffee for us both.

"You had no further children."

No.

"And there were no clues or leads. You never knew what happened to Emily."

This time she didn't respond straightaway.

"We all have our hardships to bear in this life, you know."

Mr. Smith: "Not a day goes by that I don't miss her. Not a day. 'She went missing.'"

"But we have to move on with our lives, don't we?" his wife said.

"I think we do, absolutely." I stood. "Thank you for your time, ma'am, and for the coffee."

She and I walked to the door. There, I looked back at Mr. Smith. He sat unmoving, eyes still on the blank TV screen, cup in hand. The collar of his polyester shirt was badly pilled and worn half through. Hair sprouted from his ears.

We are all, I suppose, waiting for something.

What difference could finding my parents possibly make? I'd always made light of adoptees who, coming to adulthood, insisted upon doing so. So many years have passed. Whatever congruencies and connections once may have obtained are long gone. One might as well seek out Cro-Magnon ancestors.

Mrs. Smith and I stood by the door. The final hold of day, splashes of bright orange and pink on the horizon, let go as dark seeped up from the ground. Three kids of twelve or so went by on motorized scooters. The scooters sounded like huge mosquitoes.

"On the phone you said you were doing a feature about missing children."

"That's one of the projects we're researching, yes."

"Well, I hope we haven't wasted your time, dear."

"Not at all."

She looked toward them as the kids on their scooters came back up the street. They rode abreast down the center of it. A Chevy van lugged slowly, patiently behind. Streetlights were coming on, one by one.

"We do just have to get on with our lives, don't we?"

The door was closing even as she said it.

That night as I lay in bed with the radio on, Vice President Courtney-Phillips held a press conference to announce her divorce. We have decided it is in the best interests of.

Her son, now sixteen, will be going to live with his father in Silver Spring. Daughter Amy, fourteen, will remain with her in their DC apartment. A reporter asks about rumors that she will be making a bid for president in the upcoming election.

Absolutely not, she said. A woman? A black woman? And divorced in the bargain? Who would vote for someone like that?

Me.

4

THE PHONE'S RINGING dredged me from sleep.

Two thirteen A.M. Slats of moonlight fall obliquely against the wall opposite. I hear, momentarily, the call of an owl before traffic sounds come back up to obscure it. The shadow of my hand as I reach for the phone is immense, frightening.

"Miss Rowan? Jenny Rowan? I'm sorry to bother you this time of night."

"Who is this?"

"Lisa Boudreaux. I'm a doctor at Washington Hospital Center, chief resident in surgery. I have your number from Detective Collins. You know a young woman named Cheryl, I believe?"

"I do."

"We have her here in ER. She's been assaulted and badly beaten. Detective Collins thought you would want to know."

"Raped?"

A pause. "Yes."

"Is she going to be okay?"

"Basically, yes, we think. There's a lot of damage. She's on her way to OR."

"Is Jack there?"

"Jack?"

"Detective Collins."

"He's en route."

"So am I. Please tell him that."

He stood as, twenty minutes later, I came off an elevator that opened directly onto the waiting room to which I'd been directed by the elderly man at the information desk downstairs.

"She's in surgery," he told me.

"How bad is it?"

"You know she was raped, right?"

I nodded. "Where was she?"

"MDC." The so-called Mental Diagnostic Center, usually the way station on a cruise to one or another of the local psychiatric facilities. Even had their own little kangaroo courtroom set up in there. "No one else had room for her on such short notice."

"How bad is it?"

"Besides the rape? Her face is pretty well banged up. Some broken ribs. Looks like the fingers of one hand got bent back hard, dislocated, maybe they're broken too. Could have been worse— she didn't struggle."

"Of course she didn't struggle. With her history?"

He started to say something else, stopped himself. "I'm sorry."

Doors swung open then, and a young woman in oversize scrubs stepped through. The scrubs were poor camouflage for the shape beneath or for her carriage, for the beauty of olive skin, golden eyes. She walked directly to Jack.

"Dr. Boudreaux: Jenny Rowan."

She smiled. Possibly I read more into her momentary pause, into her eye contact, than was intended.

"She's going to be okay," Dr. Boudreaux said. "Three broken

ribs, which we've taped. They're fairly stable, but she's going to be sister to pain for a while."

Pain, she was used to. Pain, she understood.

"We've splinted the hand. I put in a couple dozen stitches around her mouth and one eye. Used the finest thread I could. With luck there'll be little or no scarring."

"They did a rape kit in ER?" I asked.

"Of course."

"Thanks, Lisa."

"You're welcome." Briefly her hand, nails cut almost to the quick, touched his. "She's coming up from the anesthetic. You'll be able to see her shortly. One of the nurses from Recovery will let you know. Meanwhile, I've got to go sew up a bladder and put it back where it belongs."

"You two know one another, I see," I said once she'd gone back through the automatic doors.

"We've been out a time or two. Dinner, a movie—like that. Tried more often, but one of us is always getting reined in by our beeper."

"She's gorgeous."

Jack nodded. "We met here—where else am I going to meet someone like Lisa? Before that I'd given up dating. I'd go out with a secretary, someone who worked in a department store, there we'd be, she talking about her family or what was on TV, me sitting across from her with a smile pasted on my face thinking about the dead child we'd found stuffed into a gym bag that day, or the guy we'd had a few years back who broke into upscale homes and hammered railroad spikes into the owners' hands and feet, pinning them to the wall."

A nurse coming through the magic doors saved us further awkwardness.

"You go," Jack said.

Coming into Recovery, I faced an expanse of stretchers upon which lay perhaps two dozen huddled shapes. Some looked as immobile as sand dunes; others, either unable to do so or urged back down by staff, repeatedly tried to sit up; a couple were turned to the side, vomiting into basins. Stretchers sat nosed into service bays much like those in mechanic shops.

Cheryl tracked me as I approached. I reached for her hand, which found its way out from beneath the stained, torn, crisply starched sheet.

"Sorry, girl."

Tears swam into her eyes.

"Life's a bitch, then you die," I said. "They just forget to tell you the dying goes on for years and years, and how much it can hurt. Who did this, Cheryl?"

She shut her eyes. New tears squeezed out around the lids. They'd wash it all clean. She'd open her eyes to a better world. It hadn't worked yet, but what else was there?

"I have a list of all intakes. Just tell me who it was."

"I can trust you, right?"

"You wouldn't be asking if you hadn't already decided you can."

I stood holding her hand, listening to periodic retching and rattly coughs, to the ringing of phones, to the chatter of others at the front counter, nurses, unit secretaries, residents and interns, anesthesiologists, transporters, X-ray techs.

"He works there," Cheryl said.

Two days later Jack was waiting by lockers as Jeremy "Jerry" Dunne, Psych Tech II, arrived for work.

"You're under arrest for rape, assault, and battery," Jack said, spinning out the Miranda-Escobedo formula. A uniformed cop relieved Dunne of his backpack as Jack cuffed him.

Dunne's history was a long one. He'd begun as strong-arm orderly at the state hospital; moved from there to major abuse at two nursing homes, from both of which he'd been fired; then found employment at MDC.

"What, you don't follow up on references? Don't bother to check work history?" Jack asked. I never again saw him as angry as he was that day.

The medical director looked up from what must have been very important paperwork. "You have any idea how many positions we have to fill? How easy do you think it is to hire people at just over minimum wage? Anyone has significant experience, nine out of ten times HR's going to go ahead and process them."

"Magic 8-Ball time again," I said.

They both looked at me.

I mimicked turning the ball over in my hand. "Signs point to yes. Concentrate and ask again." Neither knew what I was talking about, of course.

"Do *you* have any idea what a piece of shit this girl's life has been, you smug asshole?" Jack said. "Drive up in your Beemer and park it in your reserved space, have a nice lunch, pull down, what? a hundred thou a year, twice that?"

"Watch yourself, Detective. Our lawyers—"

Jack's stare stopped him cold.

"You hired a man who all his life has preyed on weakness," Jack said. "Now he's about to find out how that looks from the other side. I only wish you could be there with him."

We'd walked out into ambiguous late afternoon—early evening, my favorite time of day, homing as though on instinct to a diner near the cop house. Locusts gave witness in trees outside.

"Down, boy!" I'd said back at MDC.

"I know, I know. Don't much care for doctors in the first place."

"You seemed to like Lisa Boudreaux well enough."

"True. Different species, though."

Jack shoveled a piece of coconut-cream pie into his mouth as I sipped coffee.

"There's no anger in you, is there, Jenny? None at all. I don't understand that."

"Who would you have me be angry with?"

"Your parents?"

"I never knew them."

"The man who abducted you."

"Danny? He was just being true to what he was, being Danny. He couldn't help himself. And that was many and many a year ago—"

"In a kingdom by the sea."

"Exactly. There's nothing I can do to change any of it."

"Society, then—for allowing this to happen."

"*Way* too big a bag to haul around, on such a short trip."

The waitress brought us refills on coffee, asked if we needed anything else. *Gina*, according to her name tag. Kind brown eyes, beautiful silver-gray hair cut short. Slight limp—or maybe just sore feet from all these hours on them? She tucked the check under the ashtray. Jack covered it with a twenty.

"You want it all to make sense, don't you?" I said. "Our lives, the world. Clear reasons. Explanations. Even when you know better than most how untidy the world and all our lives are."

Outside, locusts' songs had given way to the cold, silent light of fireflies. As a child we'd catch them in our hands and put them in jars with punctured lids. Lightning bugs, we called them. First time I heard about Diogenes, I had an image of him holding one of those jars high. That would be his lantern as he went about on his search.

I woke witnessing the birth of the universe.

Static on the TV screen, physicists say, is residual radiation left over from the Big Bang.

I looked around as, slowly, it came back to me.

Jack and I had adjourned to his apartment and gone on talking. He'd had three or four pours of Scotch, I'd had two. At some point he phoned for a pizza. We watched *Bell, Book and Candle* as we ate. He loved old movies and thought Kim Novak the most beautiful woman he'd ever seen. I must have fallen asleep. He must have draped the quilt over me. Not that I needed it, with weather warm and sultry. I'd promptly thrown it off.

Nice thought, though.

"You're awake. Good. I wasn't sure when you needed to be at work. Bad sleeper myself, so I can't abide waking anyone up. Coffee?"

"Please."

Steam leaked from the bathroom he'd just left, frosting the full-length mirror on the closet door alongside. He wore a red terrycloth robe from which tangles of snagged threads hung like dreadlocks.

"What time is it?"

"Little after seven. Sugar, milk?"

"What, and mess up good coffee?"

"Black it is."

Detouring to shut off the TV, he brought the coffee to me, along with my options.

"We can grab bagels at the corner or, if by some miraculous chance you have a taste for rubbery eggs and half-raw bacon, I can cook for you."

"Tough choice . . ."

"That's life."

"On the other hand, there's nothing like a bagel in the morning."

"*Good* choice." He hoisted his coffee cup in tribute. "Bathroom's yours. I laid out towels and a washcloth."

He had a fresh cup of coffee waiting when I came out. He'd changed into blue slacks, light blue dress shirt, old-style penny loafers. Back in my own clothes, body still remembering the hot shower, I'd wrapped myself in a quilt. Been a long time since my last sleepover.

"I've had that quilt since I was sixteen," Jack said. "Went to college with me, probably deserves its own BA, all the bookwork I did under its aegis."

"Aegis?" First *abide*, now this.

"What good's a liberal arts education if you can't drop in a word like that now and then?"

"And just how long have you waited?"

"Been on the tip of my tongue for, oh, fourteen years or so." His eyes lowered to the quilt, then came back to mine. "My mother made it."

"It's beautiful."

"It was half done when she went into the hospital for tests. She finished it there, while going through radiation therapy and chemo. Her doctors later admitted they knew it wouldn't do any good. She was thirty-six."

"I'm sorry, Jack."

"Don't be. She had a good life. One of those quality-over-quantity things."

Strangely, the Bagel Place was all but deserted, a single elderly man sitting with his newspaper, oxygen tank, and go-cup of coffee at the foremost of six tables inside, a pair of thirtyish men in crisp white shirts, ties, and razor-cut hair at one of the tables out front.

Jack ordered an espresso and a bagel with jalapeno cream cheese. I switched to tea, asked for plain cream cheese and capers, bagel double-toasted. Thing people don't understand, Jack said, is how much less caffeine there is in espresso than in regular coffee. It's the time the water spends in contact with the beans.

Workers, possibly management, had the radio dialed to the local NPR. The host and her daily pickup band of authorities were talking about books and whether they mattered in today's world, whether they had an effect. Do the math, one interviewee said. For every word in *Mein Kampf* a hundred and twenty-five people died. For every chapter, two hundred thousand.

5

A MONTH OR SO BACK, squatters had moved into the house next door. Boards still covered door and windows. The squatters came and went via the alley and back door, usually at night. Carefully packaging waste, by night they placed it in our neighbors' disposal bins. Ever so often I'd pack up food and take it over. There was a core group—a young man named Snake, new mother Josie, Dolly Partonish Judy-Lynn, adult runaways Buddy and Dana—with others wandering in and out of the assembly.

I walked in the back door to find Josie there in the kitchen nursing her baby.

"Pizza's here!" she said.

"Well, not exactly. But there's a bunch of tuna, canned soup, and pasta in the sack. Some bread and crackers, apples, cheese. Couple of jars of peanut butter. A gallon of milk and vitamins for you."

"Thanks, girl."

Snake, having heard Josie, stood in the doorway.

"Who'd of thought it? A good neighbor."

"Yeah, well. I've been meaning to speak with you about the yard."

"I'll get right on it. It the old tires or the three-foot-high john-songrass that bothers you?"

"The tires are a nice touch."

"Planters, like," Josie said.

"Stay and eat with us? Can't remember whose turn it is to cook—"

"You know damn well whose turn it is, Snake."

"—but it's the least we can do."

"I should get back."

"Have time for a drink, at least?"

"Okay."

He poured red wine from a jug standing on the cabinet into an old jelly jar and a chipped water glass. He handed the glass to me.

Josie cleared her throat.

"Not while you're nursing, sweetheart."

She pouted, dramatically. At the same moment, the baby threw up. That was the most movement I'd ever seen from it. Most of the time it could pass for a doll. Wiping away drool and milk with her shirtsleeve, Josie put the baby back to breast.

Snake and I clinked glasses. Well, glass and jelly jar, anyway.

"Appreciate your helping us out."

"No problem."

"Not a lot that would. Our kind's not too popular."

"You might be surprised."

"You think?" He threw back the rest of his wine. "God, how I'd like to be surprised."

6

MALLS, A LONG PIECE in today's *Washington Post* makes official, are on their way out, have been so for some time, in fact—causing me to reflect on my old homestead. High vacancy rates, low consumer traffic, a shift toward renovation of the central city, big-box stores such as Fry's Electronics and Walmart, all have taken their toll.

"They're dinosaurs," according to one expert, "as out of touch with today's consumers as rotary-dial phones and vinyl recordings. Hundreds of regional malls lie empty, gutted, abandoned. Probably ten times that number have no true reason for being."

Grayfields, he called them, for their sea-like acres of cement parking lots, harking back to the designation of old industrial sites as *brownfields.*

Roofs ripped off, sidewalks, canals, and palm trees laid in, town houses or apartment blocks added, select malls are being reworked by developers into quirky small villages. Interestingly enough, the first American malls were intended to resemble just that.

I had a good life in one of those malls. My very own world. A biosphere of sorts, where I lived in harmony with my environment.

Took food and clothing and shelter, fallen fruit, from the ground at my feet.

So much passes. With every step we take, we leave so much behind.

"Blink once and the world changes," I remember a writer saying in an interview I edited some years back. "Blink twice, *you* change."

Early one morning around the time I was editing that interview, not long after my snipe hunt for parents, I arrived at work to find that a message had been left for me. Would I please call the number below at my earliest convenience.

Doing so, I was asked please to hold.

"Miss Rowan?"

"Yes?"

"This is Dr. Duhon, at George Washington University Hospital. I'm chief resident here. You know a Daniel Taylor, I believe?"

Danny. I knew his name—I'd seen it on the dangling hospital name badge he still wore sometimes as he pulled me out from under—even if I'd misplaced my own.

"Yes."

"Mr. Taylor is currently a patient here. The details are disturbing. . . . Not that this has anything to do with my reason for calling."

I waited. Often life is like raw footage. Suspend judgment, wait, watch, witness. Let it flow through you. Give patterns time to reveal themselves. One way or another, it all gets edited. Man's a pattern-making animal—just as the writer in that interview said.

"Are you acquainted with living wills, Miss Rowan?"

I was. We'd done a documentary on them a year or so back.

"Mr. Taylor had a living will on file with his physician. As the person designated to be his agent in all matters relating to his care, he lists you."

Moments of silence on the line.

"Miss Rowan?"

"Yes."

"Would it be possible for you to come down here? The sooner the better."

"I've just this minute got in to work."

"I know. But here's the thing. Following upon massive trauma, Mr. Taylor has sustained a series of medical crises, leading his caretakers to believe that the quality of life has been irredeemably damaged, which brings his living will into high relief. Our consensus at this time is that removal of life support is the most humane option. And for that we need your consent."

Further silence.

"I realize how difficult this must be. You and Mr. Taylor were close?"

So many questions, without and within.

How had he found me, how had he learned where I lived, what name I went under? Had he been watching from afar? Why on earth would Danny name me as his guardian? He'd taken care of me, now it was my turn, the way parents and children so often reverse roles in later life?

Have to be away an hour or so, I told Mickie. Family.

I didn't think you *had* family, she said. Then when I offered nothing further, she went on: Take as long as you need. Just let me know how it's going, and if there's anything I can do.

Of course I would.

What did I expect? Danny looked so old and so fragile lying there, this man who once had shaped and cradled the whole of my world with his hands. Illness and hospitals do that. I know. Strip away masks and worldly station, peel veneer back to the cheap wood beneath, turn us from pronoun to adjective. Something from

Joyce came to me, Stephen Daedalus with one of his sad charges at the teacher's desk: "My childhood bends beside me. Too far for me to lay a hand there once or lightly."

Open yourself to it, I reminded myself. Let it flow through. That's how you live now. Let the patterns make themselves known to you.

My talent, such as it was, lay in finding connections, nothing more. Give me four hours of random film about rodeo activity, about which I know nothing, and I'll bulldog it into meaning, I'll build you a perfect two-minute world. But this time I stood there knowing that the pieces, the patterns, would not coalesce.

"On the phone, when you called," I said to Dr. Duhon, thirty-ish, cape of dark hair across her neck, face blotchy with lack of sleep, looking more like a librarian than someone shoulder to shoulder daily with illness, injury, and death, "you called the details disturbing."

"I'm not sure I should talk about this."

"Danny abducted me when I was eight years old," I said. "He kept me in a box under his bed."

Dr. Duhon's eyes focused more clearly on me. She'd been at this, what? six, seven years? Encountering, hourly, worlds she could hardly have imagined to exist.

"You weren't the only one."

"I never thought I was."

"Police found evidence of multiple kidnappings. Most of the children were released after a short time. Some he kept longer. At least one was never seen again."

I nodded. Her beeper sounded. She went to a phone on the wall to respond, spoke for a moment, and came back.

"Two months ago he took a child from Chuck E. Cheese. It was a birthday party for the girl, and a late arrival, an uncle, caught a glimpse of her as Mr. Taylor pulled out of the parking lot in a blue Ford pickup. He tried to follow, but traffic was bad.

"Two days later, this uncle's getting back in his car at an AM/PM. He's just gassed up. And when he looks to the right he sees that same truck and driver at the other line of pumps. He follows him, makes a note of the address. That night around midnight he and some friends pay a visit to Mr. Taylor. Break down the door, break his thumbs. The girl, Missy, is there. One of them takes her home, the others stick around. They're there a long time.

"That uncle's the one who called it in. Gave himself up. So far he's refused to name anyone else.

"Mr. Taylor arrived at our ER with multiple broken bones, a pneumothorax from broken ribs, blood in his urine, a concussion, one eye gouged out. Nothing we don't see every day. But sometimes, especially with trauma patients, this domino thing starts happening. By morning most of the left lung was whited out. The wound site where we'd set a compound fracture of his humerus became infected. He reacted adversely to medications. Another, opportunistic infection, MRSA, took hold. He began having arrhythmias. Then one morning around three he arrested."

I looked down at this small, withered thing on the bed, once so huge and godlike in my life. So very little left of him now. We all come to this.

"Does he know I'm here?" I asked.

"Probably not. But we can't ever be sure. It's possible that, on some level, he may be able to hear you. Would you like some time alone with him?"

"No. He's not in pain, right?"

"No. We can see to that, at least."

Turning from the empty buckets of Danny's eyes, I signed the papers Dr. Duhon tendered. Only such measures as appropriate to keep the aforesaid patient comfortable would be undertaken. There would be no mechanical life support, no attempts at resuscitation.

Turning back, I took Danny's cold hand in mine and felt myself grow larger.

Vice President Courtney-Phillips's saga continues. The divorce is under way. Her son, Reagan, reversing an earlier decision, has chosen to remain with his mother. Go figure. She's getting the kind of attention generally awarded Hollywood stars, pop singers, media arbitrators of canned-hate or feel-good shows. On a major website 41 percent of respondents say that, should she run for president, they'd seriously consider voting for her.

"Still nothing I can do to help?" Mickie asked when I called to plead the rest of the day off.

"Not really."

"Okay. I'm here till ten or eleven, as usual. After that, mostly unable to sleep—also as usual—I'll be at home."

In the car I snagged the last moments of the latest update on Vice President Courtney-Phillips before listening to a review of the newest Henry James film adaptation and a three-minute overview of Sam Cooke's ten-minute career.

Then I came home to four messages from Keith. We'd become acquainted on the phone when I called to get a sound bite on Derrida for an interview I was editing, and had since been out a couple of times.

Jenny, it's me. Had a great time last week. Hope you did too. Probably we should do it again?

Miss Rowan? Keith Kelly here. I'd appreciate a call at the earliest opportunity.

Hello? Hello? Anyone there?

Okay, I can take a hint. You never want to see me again. That being the case, I plan to throw myself off a cliff. . . . Could you please call and let me know the location of the nearest suitable cliff?

I called and set up a rendezvous at Chili's. A young woman with orange hair and a nose ring escorted me to the table. Keith had a couple of schooners of beer before him, a saucer of lime wedges alongside.

"With or without?" he said.

"Without."

One of the schooners came my way. We sat silently awhile as levels of beer fell.

"This the best you could do for a cliff?" he said.

"I don't much care for heights."

"Or for me."

"I'm sorry, Keith."

"No problem, in the grand scheme of things. I got the drift. Figure I'll just drown my sorrows in comfort food. You hungry?"

"No. But another beer would be good."

He went to the bar to get them. I thanked him. We sat nursing the schooners, smiling obliquely at one another.

"Derrida could do a whole essay on this encounter," Keith said. "What's said, what's not said."

So I told him about Danny. The expurgated version, in which

Danny became simply an avuncular friend, someone from my childhood.

"I'm so sorry, Jenny."

"Life sucks sometimes."

"One of the things it's good at. But other times it just kind of floats, like a kite, carries you up with it. The ground's down there but you don't care."

"You'd have been good for me, wouldn't you, Keith?"

"Oh dear." He smiled. A good smile from a good man. Why couldn't that be enough? "Like my French teacher back in college, the woman has galloped forth onto the terrible ground of tenses that none of us understand. Note also that she has brought up the great mystery of The Good."

Keith taught philosophy, a discipline that often seems to put uppercase letters into one's speech. By day he shadowed the dawn of Western intellect, chalking Greek and Latin on the board, invoking Heraclitus, Thales, Plato's spin on Socrates. By night he hung out in clubs where the newest music was happening. We're all such contradictions. Whitman saw that early on. About himself, about all of us. How that was at the core of whatever America was.

"I apologize," Keith said as he took in my reaction to his remark. "Irony's a poor crutch. Never fails to prop one up, though— that's the attraction."

We could spend some considerable time talking about attraction, I supposed.

"Yes. You're right. We could."

"When I was a child, I had these two tiny plastic dogs, one white, the other black." The memory had bloomed suddenly in my mind. "They were mounted on tiny magnets. Move one of the dogs close, the other would skitter away."

Keith drained his beer and stood. "Take care, Jenny."

"You as well."

Another regret pushed forward in my life? What we do, what we don't, actions, inactions. So many of them up there waiting for us, hanging out like thugs on tomorrow's street corners.

Take care, Keith had said. I took tears instead. They came into my eyes as I sat in the parking lot, engine running, radio on, with no idea what these people were talking about. Some local election. Whether or not the candidates were qualified. Soft money, smoke-filled back rooms, allegations of illegal campaign contributions. What matter, any of it? Life would go on, nothing much would change. Other young women would be abducted, other presidents would plunge us into mad, hopeless wars, the Courtney-Phillipses of this world would soon enough be forgotten, a thousand Keiths and Jennys would fail to connect.

And my tears? Were they for lost opportunities? For Keith? For Danny?

For all of us.

7

"WE CAN GO THROUGH this stuff, discard a lot of it, I figure, consolidate the rest."

"It's fine. Kind of like being in an igloo, boxes instead of ice blocks."

I hadn't been in the spare bedroom since moving in. Most of this, I had no idea what it was.

"For that matter, far as I'm concerned, we could just toss it all."

"I don't need much space, Miss Rowan."

"Jenny."

"For me, this is palatial."

Palatial.

"We can go out later, pick up whatever you need. Clothes, toothbrush, deodorant, personal goods. . . . Are you hungry?"

"A little. But if you don't mind, I'd just like to stay here awhile, enjoy the quiet."

"I understand."

"Miss Rowan?" she said when I was at the door.

"Yes?"

"Did he love you?"

I turned back.

"I don't know. Maybe. Yes."

"What was his name?"

"Danny."

"Mine was Gus."

Our eyes met. For a moment there were only the two of us, alone in the world.

"No one understands that."

"No," I said. "No reason they should. No way they can."

She nodded. Moments later her head peered around the door-jamb. The gravity was gone as quickly as it had come.

"Be okay if I take a bath?"

"Honey, this is your home, you can do anything you want."

I stood at the kitchen island listening to water run, wondering if there was anything in pantry or fridge that bore a reasonable chance of being transubstantiated into dinner.

What the hell was I thinking? I hardly knew this girl. "Twenty years old going on twelve," Jack had said. She was in pain, deep, unacknowledged pain, and would be for some time. She was like water, changing shape continually, at the least disturbance. It would take years for her character to settle and form. And in all my adult life I'd never lived with anyone.

In the bottom drawer of the refrigerator I found four lemons clinging precariously to life.

I knocked lightly on the door she'd left ajar. Cheryl was fast asleep. I set the glass of lemonade on the floor alongside the tub.

She remained asleep—though relocated from tub to bed—the next morning when I left for work. I stuck a note under a salt shaker on the island: *Coffeemaker on warm, bagel wrapped in aluminum foil and tucked away in the oven.*

Around nine, Suzie buzzed to say I had a call.

"The bagel was wonderful. Thank you," Cheryl said. "I don't drink coffee, though."

"Okay. Give it time. We're just getting to know one another."

"So dinner's on me."

"You don't have to do that."

"What time will you be back?"

"Sixish?"

Well past eight, as it turned out. Plate of wilted pickles, olives and salami, bowl of sliced tomatoes and cucumbers drizzled with vinegar and olive oil, cubes of sweating cheddar speared on round toothpicks waiting for me on the kitchen island. Cheryl waiting for me there, too. Bottle of white wine open to breathe. Two glasses. Cheryl poured and handed one to me.

"Dinner's in the oven. Staying warm, I hope."

"I'm sure it's fine. And I do apologize. I should have called."

This roommate thing was going to take some getting used to, for both of us.

"I don't mind." Her eyes met mine and glanced away. "That's a great little store."

"What store?"

"On the corner? Two blocks up?"

"Stephano's."

She nodded.

"Everyone around here just calls it the Greek's."

"Nice people."

Now that was something I hadn't heard before, surliness being more or less the stock in trade at the Greek's, right along with some of the best produce and one of the best cheese selections in the city. *Nice people?* My first intimation of the effect Cheryl had on others.

"I made a casserole, grits and cheese. Something my mother used to make, back in Texas. That and a salad. Hope it's okay."

"You know I'm vegetarian?"

"I called Officer Collins, to see if he knew what you like. He told me."

Over dinner I explained why I was late, how what everyone spoke of as The Big Story had fallen into our laps. Footage that gave new meaning to the adjective *raw* arrived in a flood: snapshots of high-school transcripts, blurred copies of high-school yearbooks and marriage certificate, establishing shots of town, school, city hall, city streets, both homes.

We're looking at an hour-long special and a probable sale to the networks here, Mickie said.

While both their wives drove Rolls-Royces and regularly showed up at society parties and civic events, Daniel Cross and Doug Crane seemed to be always away on business.

A little better than a week ago, around nine in the morning, Helen Cross had pulled into her garage. A neighbor remembered hearing the garage door going up as the Rolls idled on the driveway, waiting. That same neighbor went over around noon, when the two of them generally met for coffee. She knocked at the kitchen door, went on in. No sign of Helen, no coffee. Opening the connecting door she stepped into the garage. Helen was there, still in the driver's seat. The engine was no longer running, but only because its gas supply had been exhausted. Suits, sport coats, trousers, dresses, and dress shirts fresh from the dry cleaner lay in the back seat. We believe Mrs. Cross passed out as she pulled into the garage, before she could shut the engine off, a spokesman for the ME said, and since there's no elevation of carbon dioxide level in her blood, she almost certainly stopped breathing at that time. The autopsy disclosed a massive MI.

The day of the funeral, Daniel Cross disappeared. The front door had been left unlocked. Kitchen cabinets were thick with plates of food brought or sent by friends, and the coffeepot, though unplugged, was half full. There was no sign of struggle, police said.

With his wife of fifty years, Daniel Cross had fathered three children. One of those children was a lawyer, real estate mostly, the occasional small-business incorporation. Unsettled by the double blow of his mother's death and his father's disappearance, he began working his way through the house and his father's financial records. Two months later he stood on the porch of a pleasantly appointed house twenty miles or so away from his parents' home. A woman—Melinda Jones—answered the door. In the doorway behind her appeared his father.

Melinda Jones, it turned out, a professional woman who chose to keep her own name, had been living for some thirty years in seeming matrimony with one Douglas Crane.

And Daniel Cross and Douglas Crane were the same person.

By this time Cheryl and I had finished dinner. We stacked dishes, carried them to the kitchen.

"I can do these," Cheryl said.

"No way. You cooked, I clean. That's the rule."

"You sure?"

"I'm new at this, but yeah, I'm pretty sure."

"Okay."

She pulled one of the stools up to the island and poured another glass of wine.

"Gus always served wine with dinner. Make every day a

celebration, he said. Sometimes he wanted me to dress up for dinner, and he'd bring me these beautiful dresses. Then for weeks he'd take everything away, insist that I sit at the table naked, do the dishes naked." She took a delicate sip. "I don't know how to thank you for taking me in, Jenny."

"You don't have to."

In the stainless steel backdrop of the sink I watched my dim, distorted image scrub plates and rinse them, hand them off-frame. Have-tos and shoulds, I thought: how so many of us come to measure out our days.

"It's good to have you here," I said.

Cheryl smiled. A beautiful smile. No wonder even the folks at Stephano's treated her kindly. I was almost done with dishes. She refilled my glass.

So many in the world live this way, of course. They come home to husbands, wives, lovers or family, talk over the day, talk about nothing in particular. Even when everything inside them wants to scream or weep or cry out, they go on talking, voices low, darkness rising like black water at their windows, in their lives.

8

SOME TIME BACK, we did a documentary on mothers and daughters. Brief bios of professional women and their offspring, a woman with twelve daughters, photos and read-alouds from letters, a mother-daughter team of bounty hunters down in Tennessee. None of the profiles much over two minutes, but one of the shortest had engraved itself on my memory. A young woman went looking for the mother who'd abandoned her when she was twelve. This is in San Francisco's Tenderloin. She puts on her best dress, takes care with her makeup, her hair's freshly washed and conditioned. At the residential hotel to which she's tracked her mother she's told to check the bar around the corner. Just outside the bar there's "a heap" on the sidewalk, and the heap's wearing what the guy back at the residential hotel described. "I'm Julie, your daughter," the young woman says. "Can I help you?" The heap slowly opens one eye and takes the young woman in. "You look like a slut," she says.

I had good reason to be thinking about mothers and children.

Everything about the Cross-Crane story got dropped with news of the disappearance and possible kidnapping of Vice

President Courtney-Phillips's son. Reagan (Ray Gun to his friends) left school as usual the day before at half past three, driving the six-year-old Corsica he'd bought with his own money to the antiquarian bookstore where he'd earned that money, but he never arrived. Dialing home to check her messages, the vice president listened to a call from the store's owner, Rob Rosenfeld. Reagan had never before missed a day's work; Rosenfeld was concerned.

"I thought these kids had Secret Service protection," Mickie asked.

"They used to. I guess not anymore," said one of the researchers.

"You're looking into that, right?"

"Of course."

Now they would be.

We were all sitting around the long table in the conference room. Monitors fore and aft piped in news from the major networks, audio dialed out. Talking heads, grave expressions. Their hair was perfect.

"So what do we have?" Mickie asked.

She looked at Luis, our news director.

"Bupkis," he said.

"The head of a pin would be too big." This from his assistant. Luis came up through the ranks, OJT cameraman to editor to manager; his assistant had a degree in communications from the state university.

"Great. So we've got a basket the size of Texas and not a single egg in sight."

"Yep," Luis said.

One of the anchorpersons was scribbling in her notebook.

"Care to share, Lori?" Mickie asked.

"I was just writing down what you said."

Mickie shook her head in amazement.

"Here's the plan, then. Every half hour we come on with a spot announcement. That's it. Lori, you and Dennis put your heads together and work the spot up, twenty seconds tops. The vice president's son is missing under suspicious circumstances, blah, blah. That's it. Until we actually know something, there'll be no speculation, no background, no interviews with experts—we don't do puffed wheat."

Like a schoolchild, Luis raised his hand.

"May I be excused to work on my résumé?" he said.

"I know. I know." Mickie's eyes swept over us. "The backers and bean counters aren't going to like this."

No one spoke.

"We done here?" Luis finally said.

Mickie nodded.

"Back to our jobs, then," Luis said. "While we still have them."

For me, until we had more on the boy's disappearance, the big story of Cross-Crane now having gone small, that meant getting back to the Helton affair, i.e., trying to find some way to make viewers sit through three to four minutes about the controversy over which versions of a mostly forgotten film star's movies would be burned onto DVDs and thereby immortalized. Studios had done their own cuts at release, but there was no archive of these. Who could have imagined the future would care? (No one was at all sure it did.) Back then studios ground this stuff out and put it on the road. Extant reels had been cut and spliced by two or three generations of projectionists, either to conform to time or gloss over lost frames. Hoping to be remembered, in his final years the star had ordered up his own versions, paying for them out of pocket.

Unfortunately he'd left behind no will and six children who couldn't agree on so much as today's date.

So he *was* remembered, and would have another spark of fame, albeit for the controversy and not for his movies.

What I came up with was intercutting discussion of the controversy, plus interviews with his children and reminiscences from fellow actors, with brief scenes from the star's movies that reflected back on what had just been said. A couple of times the overlaps were spooky, *way* too close to the bone; a couple more were funny as hell.

Straw into gold. I'd taken a dull story and turned it into this small, polished wonder. That's what Mickie said, anyway, right after she viewed the rough cut and said Holy shit!

And here I figured I'd just found a way to kick a dead horse back up on its feet for one last quick run.

"It's a pretty obvious idea," I said.

"Ideas are worthless. What this is about is the things you've chosen, the way you've put them together. Individually, they're nothing. Together . . . We're not going to have you much longer, are we?"

"You'll have me as long as you want me."

Smoky gray eyes met mine and held. "You're an exceedingly strange person, Jenny Rowan."

"No," I said. "I'm not."

The story broke three hours later, Lori's twenty-second spot having run five times in the interim. It was indeed a kidnapping. A group of evangelical Christians ("We are soldiers for God") claimed to have him. What did they want? Not money. ("We're well funded, thank you.") But they were concerned, mortally concerned, that America had strayed from its moorings. No one who read the Constitution could fail to recognize that it was little more than a mirror image of the Ten Commandments. We had to get back to basics. That's what Jesus wanted.

"Okay. I'm scared now," Mickie said.

"Before you ask—we tried," Luis said. "Jesus wasn't returning calls."

"So where are we going with this?" the station manager asked. I couldn't remember his ever before having put in an appearance at the conference table.

"Has anything like this happened before?" Mickie asked.

"There's nothing in our files," Luis said. "I've got Sam and Lee hitting all the major databases."

"Evangelical Christians? What are they going to do if their demands aren't met—baptize him?"

"Christians are scary."

"No scarier than anyone else trying to tell others how they have to live."

"I'm Catholic," Luis said.

"We need a special, broadcast-ready within the hour," the station manager announced, holding up a hand to ward off the protestations that began immediately. "Not me, folks. Word came down the line. From the top."

"We'll have something," Mickie said. "It'll be crap, but we'll have it."

So we went to work. This time I remembered to call and let Cheryl know I was going to be late. As I hung up, the first material started coming in from researchers.

Work is good. I understand how few people manage to find their way to work that they love, and how fortunate I am to have done so. When I think about this, I always remember a man back

67

at Westwood Mall. He had to be pushing fifty and there he was, minding the grill at a Greek fast-food place. But every sandwich he turned out, every plate of fries, every salad, it was like this was the only one, the one he'd be known by. He took that great a care. I remember him standing by the grill in slower moments looking out, watching people seated on the arcade as they ate his food, and smiling. Even then, stupid and eleven years old, I knew enough to know that he was a man to be envied.

It turned out that the religious far right had nothing to do with it, of course—just a crackpot group making the claim to draw attention to the nation's spiritual and moral shortcomings—and we wound up junking a lot of the work we did that day and night. Not uncommon in a newshawk's life. Things like that happen when you're hanging out at the edge of the world watching.

9

IT WAS 3:52 A.M. and dark as the inside of a sheep's stomach, not a star in sight, when I came streaming out of the sky and crashed onto my bed. Sound of splintering trees, screech of metal, steam rising. In the distance a bird, perhaps a monkey, screeches tentatively. One by one the jungle's noises start up again.

I'd been hard at the loom, weaving truckloads of videotape, still photos, fragments of documentaries, and archived newscasts into digital information. We now had three thirty-minute spots on Vice President Courtney-Phillips, the kidnapping, and religious fundamentalism. Rough spots, but they'd do.

"Go home, get some sleep," Mickie told me.

"Hey, I slept through most of that last edit."

One of two phones stashed in her blazer pockets rang. She answered, listened, broke the connection.

"What about you?" I asked.

"I never sleep much anyway. An hour or two and I'm okay—and I can do without that. Two or three days from now, I'll start worrying about it."

Mickie had taken what the researchers and techs gave her

and done preliminary cuts before passing them on to me for the edit. But my chief contribution was a composite of prior interviews with Courtney-Phillips. At one point Mickie stood in the doorway watching as I ran old interviews on four screens, jotting notes; after a moment she shook her head and left. The result looked good. If it hadn't been for background, clothing, and hairstyle changing from frame to frame, you could easily believe it was a single extended interview. We'd have to run a disclaimer.

Less than an hour after my head hit the pillow I was awake again. When I opened my eyes, swirling images gave way to elemental language: phrases and strings of words that bore no connection or meaning. Then these cohered to thought.

Moonlight fell in a slant, a slab of marble, across the bottom half of my bed. For a moment I had the irrational fear that when I tried to move my legs they'd be held in place. Outside the window the silhouette of a tree stood, like something cut from black construction paper and pinned against the night.

I closed my eyes again and lay perfectly still. Looking for that ever rarer sense of safety. Hoping to find, even for a moment, passage out of myself and into the world. Sometimes I can still recapture that, still manage it.

But not tonight.

How long had it been?

A change in the quality of light caused me to open my eyes. Cheryl stood hesitantly in the doorway.

"I heard what happened. With the vice president's son. Reagan?"

"Reagan, right. We don't really have anything more, at this point."

"I knew that's what you were working on, why you weren't home."

I patted the edge of the bed. She came and sat.

"I couldn't sleep either. Can I get you anything?"

I shook my head.

"Jack Collins came by earlier. To see how I was doing, he said."

"He's a sweetheart."

"He said to tell you hello. You should call him, Jenny."

Outside, a helicopter flew just above rooftop level. Its searchlight swept across the yard and struck the tree, bringing it to sudden, startling life, then moved on.

"I will."

"Good."

We tried again for sleep but within the hour found ourselves sitting across from one another at the red-topped table in my red-and-white kitchen drinking tea. We could still hear the helicopter thwacking back and forth in the distance—or maybe it was another—as daytime sounds, passing cars, chittering, insistent birds, a neighbor dragging his recycle bin out to curb, began to aggregate.

"What do I do, Jenny?"

"What we all do. Put together a life for yourself. You're just getting a late start."

Cheryl turned her face back from the window.

"I'm supposed to be making life decisions, right? So I go to Stephano's with a list of things to pick up and half an hour later I'm still standing there by the condiments. There are three dozen kinds of pickles on the shelves, a dozen different breads. I can't decide what kind of pickles to buy, can't choose a loaf of bread, but I'm supposed to plan the rest of my life?"

"But you did it, you did decide, that's the thing. And it was a great meal."

Before she ducked back out of sight, I caught a momentary glimpse of the twelve-year-old peeking from within.

"Thanks, Jenny."

"More tea?"

"Sure."

I drained the pot. She dumped three spoons of sugar into her cup.

"Ever watch a bird build its nest?" I said. "It's got part of a vine, a clump of matted hair, maybe a piece of cloth, some twigs and grass, God knows what else. But somehow it all gets plaited together, turns into this place she lives. That's what we all do—it's no different."

Cheryl finished her tea and went back to bed, again. I called in to let the station know I'd be late. Mickie answered, saying there was no way she'd expected me till afternoon if at all.

"Tell me you haven't been there all night."

"Tell *me* you got some sleep."

"Why are you answering the phone? Where's everyone else? Where's Grace?"

"Everybody else is just about where you are, one way or another. Lost between. As for Grace, her husband went bad again last night, he's back in the hospital."

"Grace?"

"Okay, I think. Not like she hasn't been through this before."

"She's at home?"

"With the phone off the hook. Her daughter's on the way in from Iowa. I had a bunch of food sent over."

"What time is it, anyway?"

"Hell, I don't know. Coming on nine?"

"I'll be in within the hour."

"No hurry. We're pretty much on automatic here. The first two spots you put together have aired twice. Response is phenomenal."

"What about the third one?"

"On hold. Sources now suggest that the kidnapping claim was fraudulent."

Try as I might, I couldn't remember a single thing about the mini-documentary on religious fundamentalism I'd assembled only hours ago.

"Anything more?"

"Nothing we credit."

I showered, slid into black jeans and a sweatshirt with a picture of Rimbaud on it, well-worn hiking boots I'd bought the day I got my GED. Hair tied back and keys in hand, I checked on Cheryl, who was sound asleep, and put food on the back steps for the neighborhood cat who came to visit most days. Snake was slipping in next door with a package of Snuggies; I waved. Stopped for a banana muffin and coffee at Sweet Beans, a local hangout for cops; then, after starting the car, turned off the engine and went back in to order two dozen bagels and assorted spreads. We've all been trampled underfoot. We're all just kind of wandering around. Neighborhood cat or news pro, someone's gotta put food out on the steps for us.

Bloated and blimplike, the day went by in a blur of empty updates via e-mail and fax, talking heads on national and local stations, snippets of NPR's *Morning Edition* and *All Things Considered* caught on the run, plow-down-sillion finishing work on a number of upcoming spots. Fine cuts and sauces might be in the offing; meanwhile our audience required its meat and potatoes.

Around three I called Jack Collins. An operator or receptionist answered and put me on hold. I'd almost given up when Jack's voice came on the line, replacing what sounded awfully like a commercial Hawaiian take on Schoenberg.

"Miss Rowan. WAAT, isn't it? I'm afraid I have no comment for the press."

"Good—since the press isn't looking for a comment."

"Hang on, Jenny." He spoke to someone there by him: a rapid, coded exchange. "Sorry again."

"No problem."

"I've been calling. Spoke to Cheryl last time out. She tell you?"

"She told me."

"I knew you'd be crazy busy, too. With all this."

"You're right. Been a rough couple of days for all of us."

"That it has."

"And I really don't want to just go on working with the hammer down, getting home halfway into the next day to eat shit for food and half pass out, then go back in for more of the same."

"Perfectly understandable."

"Thought maybe you and I could meet after work, have a drink somewhere."

"Presumptuous of you. But if by some chance you got hungry, I *might* even be willing to spring for dinner. Have to check at the ATM first, of course, be sure I have funds."

"Always push it, do you, Collins?"

He laughed. "Guess I do. I was six weeks early—just not willing to wait, my mother said. Started college the summer after I graduated from high school at seventeen, finished my degree in two and a half years."

"Whoa!"

"Took the detective's exam the very day I qualified and passed.

Full-tilt boogie, as a friend of mine, a Southerner, put it. So maybe it's time for a whoa."

He was waiting outside the station a little after six. Gray slacks, blue blazer, open-neck pearl-gray shirt. Rubber mask of Nixon looming above.

"One of your heroes, I take it."

He tugged off the mask and threw it into the back seat where, collapsed upon itself, its smile became obscene.

"Not really. Interestingly enough, it's a hands-down favorite among robbers."

Shutting my door, he leaned down to the open window.

"Is this pushing, too?"

"Absolutely. But it's a nice push. Where are we going?"

To a neighborhood bar, as it turned out, Billy's Daylight Lounge, owned and run by a retired cop though inhabited by locals. Walls hung with photos of patrons in police blue and military dress. American flags everywhere, even perched atop the toothpicks.

"White wine."

"Bourbon, beer back."

Though neither of us had anything material to offer or add, we talked for a while about the kidnapping, then over nachos and second drinks fell to serious negotiations. Collins could pay for the drinks and nibbles, no problem there, but I insisted on handling dinner.

"We're not too far from my apartment," he said.

"And how far from a grocer?"

"Three, four blocks."

"On the way?"

"Could be."

"There it is, then. We stop off, pick up food, go on to your place, and I fix dinner for us."

An hour later we sat balancing plates of pasta primavera on knees. The couch and coffee table took up most of his front room. Against the opposite wall, a span of maybe two yards—you could all but reach out and fingerprint the screen—one of his favorite movies showed on TV. Black and white. *The Best Man.*

"This is great," Jack said.

"The food?"

"All of it."

"I agree."

Wind rattled the window. As we looked that way, rain broke, slamming in bucketfuls against the pane. Henry Fonda mounted an escalator, peering down at the unexceptional man who was now to be president. Their eyes met.

"Gets to me every time," Jack said.

I looked around. Couch, table, and TV precisely placed, books squared on the coffee table, sections of the morning paper neatly stacked, blue tile coasters. I remembered remarking, when we first met, something overly neat and maybe a little compulsive about him. Jack's world, here at least, was in order. Which was about as much as any of us can reasonably hope for.

By then I think we'd hit something of an impasse. We had no store of previous conversations, no personal history to rehearse and update, which is what often passes for conversation, and neither of us was much of a storyteller. Worse, each was so private a person as to make us reluctant to ask leading questions of the other. We sat in silence, not an uncomfortable silence, for we hadn't the gift for that either, discomfort I mean, looking out at the rain.

When the buzzer broke silence, *I* broke into laughter.

"It sounds like an old man snoring!"

A short in the wiring, apparently. The buzzer would sound, drop away, start hesitantly up, quit again.

"No one comes here," Jack said, "so I never think about getting it fixed."

He stepped over my legs to get to the door. A young woman in jeans and T-shirt stood there. Clothes and hair were drenched. A pool of water spread from her feet, as though she were a toy soldier on a base. Briefly her eyes glanced past Jack to take me in. Then she looked back at him.

"Hi, Dad," she said.

10

"I'M SORRY."

"Me too."

"It was a good evening."

I'd skedaddled shortly after Deanna's appearance. Now it was noon the following day and we were having lunch at a Middle Eastern restaurant around the corner from the studio. Starting life as a specialty-food store, Open Sesame had never fully embraced its identity as restaurant. The air was alive not only with the odor of frying foods and rich coffee but also with that of the olives, feta, felafel, canned goods, lentils, teas, and spices sold in quantity from bins in the back and from the shelves that crowded every wall.

"She okay?"

"For a sixteen-year-old, yeah."

I can't do it anymore, Deanna had told him, moments after showing up at the door. Jack was helping her dry off with a blue towel; the seams had all unraveled. I hate school, I hate that stupid plaid skirt, I hate fucking (here a sharp glance from her father) violin lessons, and I hate Roberto.

Roberto?

Mom's boyfriend.

What she wanted to do, she told Jack, was come live with him. She'd get a job, study on her own for her GED. Figured then she'd put in a year at a community college before leapfrogging to a *real* college.

"She could do all that?" I asked.

"With one arm tied behind her back."

"And would?"

"If she says."

"Another pusher."

"Afraid so."

Jack bit into a felafel, steam breaking about his lips. He scooped up cucumber and tahini sauce with the remaining half.

"When I was a kid?" he said. "I remember looking around, on the bus, in study hall, in the lunchroom. Thinking how great it would be just to be like those others, not feel apart, be able to float through it all."

"We all feel special when we're young. Singled out."

"Did you?" Then the full weight of what we were saying hit him and he added, "I'm sorry."

"Yeah, not much childhood there. But feeling special . . . Yes, absolutely."

By long habit I sat with my back to the wall, watching the entrance. When the door swung wide, I said, "Excuse me."

"Girlfriend!" Kimmie and I hugged. "Join us?" One of her companions was Korean and though (as I later learned) in her thirties, looked to be little more than a child. The other was a fiftyish Caucasian, hair dyed dark brown. Standing seemed to cause her pain, but it was pain she'd patently lived with a long time, pain she rarely thought of.

"I'm with someone."

When Kimmie looked past me, her eyes went immediately to Jack. He smiled. She smiled back.

"Then your lunch, at least, is on me."

"You don't—"

She held a finger to her lips. It was altogether possible that Kimmie owned a share of the restaurant, at the very least kept their books, did their taxes.

"Call me, Jen. My little brother is engaged. We're having a quiet celebration next weekend, just family and close friends."

Which meant a hundred or more people and food enough for twice that. The yard would be solid with folding tables, chairs, coolers of beer and fruit drinks, exquisitely dressed children, the house's entryway paved with cast-off shoes.

"My parents would love to see you. Please come, Jen. And bring your friend."

"I'll do my best. Give my congratulations to Ken."

"Of course."

"So you've got a new roommate," I said after rejoining Jack and telling him about Kimmie.

"Looks like."

"You talked to her mother?"

"This morning."

"And?"

"Your basic sturm und drang. Deanna's *my* daughter, You're hardly ever home, What do you know about young women. . . . Righteous outrage aside, things have been going poorly in the household for some time. For everyone. Once she wound down, she agreed we'd give it a try."

"Anything I can do to help, let me know."

"Count on it."

Back at the studio before settling into work, I did my habitual broken run past a list of online news services. Amid tales of corporate greed, stayed executions, political defections, and puff pieces for athletes and film stars, an eight-line report from Florida caught my attention. A two-year-old girl had survived for nearly three weeks, alone in the apartment, when her mother was jailed. The girl had eaten condiments, raw rice and pasta. When found, she was covered with dried ketchup, curled up in her baby's bathtub in the apartment's tiny bedroom.

I pasted the story into an e-mail to Mickie, adding: *Could make a good spot. We have a stringer on tap down there?* She came back minutes later with *Done*, and we had footage a few hours later. Cheryl and I watched it that night. Mickie had slotted it in after an update on the kidnapping, as the closing story. I looked over and saw tears on Cheryl's face, above the bowl of popcorn.

After dinner I threw a bunch of food in an old Trader Joe's sack and went to check on the squatters.

Snake, who had taken his name after seeing John Carpenter's *Escape from New York*, unloaded each item lovingly and placed it on shelves he and his housemates had assembled from boards and random bits of furniture, cement blocks, and bricks. Kind of a Cubist's notion of shelves: seen simultaneously from multiple angles and perspectives. And the unloading was a kind of mantra.

"Progresso soups—the best."

"Tuna—capital!"

"Veggies."

"More veggies!"

"Crackers. If only—"

"And there it *is*. Cheese!"

"Canned milk. Excellent."

"Sardines."

"Green beans."

"Peanuts!"

Against a back wall Josie nursed her baby. The baby was a frightening sight, as I knew from past visits; looked like dolls for the Day of the Dead. But then so did Josie, making it a toss-up as to whether the baby's appearance resulted from its harsh environment and deprivation or simple heredity.

Sometimes I think all I've learned, the single thing I know, is the importance of letting people get on with their lives. However wretched those lives may be or we think them, much of the time it's only when others turn up hell-bent on change—family, peers, people with religious, social, or political agendas—that it all goes to shit. We're adaptable creatures. We make do. We wear the shirts we have.

From farther back in the cave, other squatters acknowledge me. Their form of thanks.

Little Jeanne, who imagines that her Midwest banker husband has, pinned to the wall by his Coffee Master, her likeness from a years-old milk carton.

Buddy, whose father traded shares in offshore drilling for controlling shares in early information technology and now each morning (Buddy is sure of this) sits on the grid of the Internet looking for sunspots: Buddy activity.

Dana, her craving for crack cocaine having supplanted an earlier taste for upscale smelly cheeses, now preferring stacked mattresses and whoever she wakes beside to custom beds and her upstate New York family.

Judy-Lynn, late of Deep South trailer parks, trailing the heritage of same. Jeans cut to show crescents of buttock, shirts tied waist-high. Big hair in sore need of care.

"You guys doing okay?" I asked.

"We'll make it."

"We always do."

"One way or thother."

"Do you know who's president?" I asked Little Jeanne. A strand of canned spaghetti—Snake had opened the can and passed it down the line—hung out the side of her mouth. She shrugged.

I looked at their faces. Each a world unto itself.

"President Burke. He's trying to help you, all of you."

"Good for him."

"Good for us."

"Like some suit's speeches in Deecee are gonna make a difference in our life."

"What, you want your fucking food back?"

"You want my baby too?" Josie said. She held it out. Its limbs swung loosely, no sign of muscle tone. Eyes unblinking.

"Look . . ." I said. A neighborhood newspaper got stuffed in the handle of my front door every other week. The latest issue was triumphant over a cause it had been espousing for months. "I came to tell you something. This building's being condemned. The city is going to tear it down. Where will you guys go?"

Snake's eyes met mine.

"Where we always go," he said. How was it possible that I didn't know this, his eyes asked. "Somewhere else."

11

"POOR'S NOT A TAG you hang on someone and it's there for the rest of their lives, like Hester's scarlet *A*. Thirty-four percent leave poverty behind within three months of entering it. One out of seventeen people at poverty level go on to become rich people. Economic mobility, opportunity—what America is all about."

"Kind of scary she has those numbers so close to hand," Mickie said.

We were watching a news conference with Candace Brocato, conservatism's current spokesman, apologist, and hired gun. Harvard grad, ex-Yale professor, author of the best-selling *Economics for Normal Folk*, frequent visitor to her family, who ran a bait shop and fishing dock back in Holly Grove, Missouri.

"Scary enough that we're sitting here watching it."

"Research."

"Right."

I glanced up to see Luis standing just outside, making frantic come-here signals. We went out into the studio's main room, where chaos ruled. Luis nodded to the bank of overhead screens monitoring major networks, CNN, local stations. Six of them. All with versions, now, of the same thing. The American people were going to be pissed that their soaps and game shows and Judge Whatsits had been tossed overboard.

There'd been a raid, it seemed, on an abandoned warehouse in Silver Spring. The FBI had received a tip, one of several hundred via their hotline as of ten A.M., suggesting that Vice President Courtney-Phillips's son might be held there. To this particular tip, for reasons withheld, they gave credence. An FBI SWAT team and a special task force from the Secret Service had gone in. Signs of recent habitation were in evidence, NBC's anchorwoman said: mattresses, bins of water, fast-food containers, canned food, packaged waste. Another anchor reported the finding of a ragged copy of *The Catcher in the Rye*—which Reagan had been reading for school.

"Damn," Mickie, Luis and I said, pretty much in unison.

"At this time there are no further leads," CNN's anchor informed us. "Crime units are at the scene, while both local and federal law-enforcement agencies remain on full alert 24/7. Stay tuned for all the latest."

The phone rang.

"That's going to be Duane," Mickie said. The station manager. "Wanting to know how we missed out on this."

"Precognition?" I asked.

"Years of experience."

"For you," Luis told her. "Line five."

She picked up the phone, listened, and hung up. It was a quirk of hers that everyone had gotten used to, I guess. She carried on entire phone conversations in which she never said a word.

"He has to get in the call to me before *he* gets the call," Mickie said. "Closer to the real, we'd call it pecking order. Here, it's management strategy. What they learn in all those weekend retreats."

"Such cynicism."

"Subtext is where the real information hides."

I held up both palms in mock surrender.

"Speaking for the moment of real," Mickie said, "how's Cheryl?"

"Okay, I think. I found college catalogs on the shelf by the tub this morning—she's a championship bath taker."

"Plans on the horizon, you think?"

"Who knows? Could just be storm clouds."

Over the next several hours, divots of new information came off the green with each putt. The ratio was something like one to ninety: for every hour and a half of coverage, maybe a minute of authentic information.

Authentic. I worried that I'd caught a case of special vocabulary, the worst sort of contagion.

We think we're communicating, Mickie told me once over lunch, we insist that in our culture we're communicating continuously, but for all the constant noise and the clamor of media in our lives it's still mostly smoke and mirrors. We have all these special vocabularies, professional, ethnic, personal—with just enough overlap to allow us to convince ourselves we share a common language. We talk and talk, make shadows on the wall with our hands, when all we're really doing is bouncing the ball from flipper to flipper, trying to keep it up there, trying to keep it in play as long as we can.

12

YEARS AND YEARS AFTER, with that shock of recognition said to be a hallmark of great literature, I came across Swinburne's lines

The four boards of the coffin lid
Heard all the dead man did

and shivered, thinking how old Algernon was so right and so wrong at the same time. He got the sense of having been at a stroke sundered from the phenomenal world, got that closure, claustrophobia, containment. But he never guessed, he'd never be able to guess, what the dead man did in there.

I can't often recapture it myself, and then but piecemeal, though memory of it, the surety of it, never leaves me. Its bright shadow touches everything I do, everything I see, everything I am.

What I was just then, late evening on a Friday, was bone tired and hungry in equal measure. Cheryl wasn't home, something that would doubtless become of major concern to me once I'd had sleep and, say, a tuna sandwich. I pulled a ratty copy of *The*

Catcher in the Rye off the shelf and fell asleep holding it in both hands, like a lily, against my chest. At some point Jack Collins called. Afterward I could remember nothing of whatever conversation we might have had.

What you are in there is eternally *in between*, neither awake nor asleep yet dreaming, not of this world nor yet quite out of it, half observing the world, half re-creating it.

A man carrying flowers home to his wife on their thirtieth anniversary is killed on the street by teenagers for the eighteen dollars left in his wallet. One of the gang members presents the flowers to his new girlfriend.

A hundred and nine people are lost when, heavy rains collecting on a flat, ung 有ttered roof, an apartment house in Pakistan collapses.

The charismatic leader of the current regime in New Olgate sees the artillery shell that is his fate bearing down on him and opens his arms wide to embrace it.

About to relieve a subdural hematoma, the neurosurgeon, who has felt poorly all day, himself suffers an aneurysm. In that last ten seconds before he falls, before there's no longer oxygen to drive the synapses, the saw in his hand continues its ordained task, slicing away much of the patient's cerebellum.

A ten-year-old feeds his baby sister her bottle just as Mother, who is at work, instructed, carefully burps her, then wraps her in a warm blanket and throws her from the window.

An elderly gentleman stops on the interstate to give assistance to a young woman whose car has stalled and, attempting to siphon traffic around, is struck by a pickup and dragged almost to the next exit. Where is my cane? he asks when the paramedics arrive, Where is my cane? As they look down at what is left of his legs.

The phone rang—a second time, a third? Taut line pulling me back to shore.

Still awash in fragments of dreams, I shuddered.

"Yes?"

"Turn on your TV." Mickie.

"Our channel?"

"Any channel." And she was gone.

The TV being an eighty-dollar knockoff special and seldom used, there was a gap between striking flint and getting fire, and when the picture came up, it was as though it bloomed from screen's bottom, starting small and growing as it rose, like dialogue balloons in comics.

Later I would wonder if my dreams had somehow been spooky premonitions.

It was the very stuff of high drama and high ratings: the elephant chain of dark limos on the freeway, Secret Service agents spilling from vehicles and spreading across parking lot and grounds, helicopter thwacking away out of sight, shuffle of the crowd assembling behind hastily set traffic barricades.

The anchor appears. His suit fits superbly. There is no wildness in his eye; everything is under control. "Here is what we know," he says.

Which means they know next to nothing.

And yet there is all this space to fill. So they go on, rolling the few solid crumbs back and forth in their mouths, spinning the web out ever thinner, long pan, split screen, reporter on the scene, authority on CVAs speaking by phone from his office at Brigham Young—trusting that all the fast footwork will distract us from thoughts that the big glittery bag has nothing inside.

President Burke, dining at a local restaurant with Justice Daniels and a childhood friend, had lifted his fork before him as though to make a point, stopped speaking, stared at the fork for a moment, and collapsed. Secret Service agents were at his side before he hit the floor, the restaurant cleared within minutes, the caravan in motion soon thereafter to George Washington University Hospital, where a crack team of trauma specialists waited.

Now President Burke lay in there (insert long shot of the ER dock and entryway), his fate in the hands of, etc.

Though unspoken, etceteras were much in evidence. Boil it down to pot's bottom, the whole spectacle was little more than one long etcetera.

Almost everyone, naturally, had a theory, guess, surmise, or conjecture free for the asking. Stroke, myocardial infarction, food poisoning, Satan, aneurysm, terrorism, a new virus.

Days later, when the story broke—that President Burke had a congenital heart condition, the fact of which had been kept securely under wraps—the conspiracy jockeys had a long run with it. I've always suspected such passionate scrambling after threads of influence to be another side of religiosity, a hunger for clear explanations (however befuddled they in fact are) in a world governed by chance.

The phone rang again and I picked it up.

"Well?" Mickie said.

"Damn."

"That about says it."

"We need to address this tonight?"

"I'm here already. Luis is on his way. Don't think there'll be much before morning, just endless recycles."

"See you in the morning, then."

Later I woke to the sound of Cheryl sobbing. Only then did I realize that in my sleep I'd heard the front door, heard her quiet and careful steps, had known that she was standing silently by my open bedroom door.

I went to her doorway now. She was sitting by the window, looking out.

"You okay?"

"I saw him, Jenny."

"Saw who?"

"Gus."

"You can't have, Cheryl. He's dead."

"I know."

"But you still think you saw him."

"It all came back."

"I'm sorry."

She turned her face from the window. Not to meet my eyes, only to gaze at the lamp on the table beside her bed, which had flickered. She reached out to tighten the bulb.

"I don't know if I'm sorry, or what. I don't know what I feel."

"That's because there's so much of it."

"So much of what?"

"Feeling."

After a moment she nodded.

"Will this go on happening?"

"I don't know," I told her. "We're all different."

I sat on the bed, close enough easily to touch her, though I didn't.

"For what it's worth," I said, "here's what I think. At some point we realize that it's not going to just happen, that we're going to have to make the decision to become human and put some effort into it. Most start young as a matter of course. Others, people like you and me, we have good reason for being late starters. But the struggle's the same. We work at making a self for most of a lifetime, only to find that the self we've created is inseparable from the struggle."

The lamp flickered again.

"Maybe I should unplug it? There could be a short."

She did, and darkness came up around us. Though in a city, of course, there's little enough true darkness. I sat watching her face in the mingle of streetlight and moonlight that spilled in the window. Headlights from a passing car lifted her features into sudden relief, then were gone.

"I should probably try to get some sleep now," she said.

"Good."

"Jenny?"

At the door I turned back.

"You said earlier that we're all different. But we're all the same, too."

"We are. Both."

"Dollars," an administration spokesman was saying as, back in my own bedroom, I turned on the radio, "are the hard currency of principle." How this related to the president's illness I had no idea, but obviously it did. Everything did, that night, that week. The stock market stood on the high board pinching nostrils shut before its dive. I had kindly thoughts for Sarah Courtney-Phillips, who I'm sure wished she'd had the decent good sense to get out of Dodge before it came to this.

It's *all* economics, Karl Marx insisted. Everything is water if you look long enough, poet Robert Creeley said.

13

WATER MANIFEST: such quantities of it that I'm unable to see past the windowpanes it runs down.

Following upon two hard-won hours of further sleep, morning also brings, besides the rain, the harder though hardly unanticipated news that, yes, President Burke is dead, dead after heroic measures at George Washington University Hospital. At the studio, myself half dressed, Luis and Mickie and much of the staff looking like refugees from some undisclosed war, we witness the swearing-in of Sarah Courtney-Phillips.

"How much weight can one person bear?" Luis said.

"And this is who's running our country," one of our two anchors said.

"There's no better educator than pain," Mickie said. "No better leveler."

Her eyes met mine. I wondered, not for the first time, if she might know more about my past than she'd ever let on.

"The networks are all over this," Luis said. "They've got everything we don't. Clearance, privilege, hordes of stringers. Money."

"They don't have Jenny. Or her thirty-minute piece on

Courtney-Phillips. And they don't have you, who's about to recut Jenny's piece with a new intro. The magic goes on."

"Presto," Luis said. Briefly, blink and you'd miss it, the two of them smiled at one another. They had a bond few of us would ever attain. Sea meeting shore. Sulfur rubbing up against potassium nitrate. That kind of bond.

Retreating to my safe room of screens, dials, and control boards, I sat watching revamps of the swearing-in. Grace brought in coffee and, when I asked after her husband, told me he was still in the hospital. "I think he'd rather be there now."

"I'm sure he wouldn't."

"You don't know Jeb. Nothing he hates so much as feeling a burden. 'I didn't mean to take over your life,' he told me last week. 'I only meant to *be* your life.'"

On one of the screens opposite us, Sarah Courtney-Phillips, asked about her son's abduction, opens her mouth only to find no words there. Her speechless, stunned face hangs in suspension.

"And here I am whining about *my* problems," Grace said.

Grace left, and I sat watching rain beat at the window. It came in tides: fists, fingertips, tiring open hands, fists again. Past the rain I could make out nothing of the larger world. Behind me, on multiple monitors, small portions of that world hung suspended for a moment in high resolution, sharply defined, then gave way to others. I turned to them, on one of which the newly appointed president pro tem of a tiny African state held forth. His chains of prefabricated Communist rhetoric were like echoes of a thunder long since passed overhead.

It's not hatred, ignorance, greed, or blind nationalism that will end our world, I often think, but some system of ideas too dearly held. The idealogues, those who go on insisting upon simple solutions, who believe that the world in all its marvelous variety must be put up in a single jar of preserves—they'll put an end to us all.

That was a pale, stumbling Saturday. Days then in which we ran off coffee, adrenaline, general ruckus and rumor, trying as newsmen to fund the checks overwritten, waiting for the world to resettle.

Two weeks after, I walked in to find Cheryl talking on the phone, many *Yes ma'am*s involved. She looked up and held out the phone. "It's for you."

"Jenny Rowan?"

Not Mickie's voice as I'd expected, but familiar nonetheless.

My turn for the *Yes ma'am*.

"This is Sarah Courtney-Phillips, Jenny. I'm calling from home, on my personal line."

Not that either of us, though we pretended, had much faith that our conversation wasn't being overheard. Later she'd tell me how it hardly seemed her home anymore. She was rarely there, and when so, was surrounded by polite strangers in dark suits. "Like a reef of coral."

Six days earlier I'd sat at the desk and, in three minutes flat, written a letter to her, taking still less time to reconsider before sending it.

Dear Mrs. President:

My name is Jenny Rowan. Rowan is adopted from all those Russian poems in which rowan trees seem so magical, Jenny is what I was called when I was young. I have worked for eight

years as news editor for station WAAT. If you wish, I can pro-
vide my supervisor's name and contact number. Years ago you
may have heard of me as Mall Girl. When I was eight, I was
abducted and kept for two years in a box beneath my abductor's
bed. His name was Danny. Escaping, I lived, as it were, off the
land—in Westwood Mall, eating discarded food, dressed in
abandoned clothing. From hunted to gatherer.

All my life I have felt at one and the same time an exception
from ordinary life and a deep kinship with all those others passed
over, relegated, forgotten. With much the same emotions, not to
mention great reluctance and trepidation, I approach you now.
If by some slim chance this reaches you, and should you feel the
scarcest tug of kinship and want someone to talk with, please get
in touch.

"A glass wall's come up between myself and the world I used to live in," she would tell me. "I can see what goes on out there, the sounds reach me, but all I'm able to feel when I put my hand against the glass is the simple heat of it." That was further along, well after this first phone call.

"Thank you for your letter, Jenny. Though I have to say that such impulsiveness hardly seems your style."

"Message in a bottle. I'm surprised it reached you."

"Surprise is still possible."

"Less and less seems to be. I take it there's no further news of your son?"

"Every lead's being actively pursued, they tell me."

"I wish you the best, ma'am. I wish you surprise."

"Thank you." She was silent a moment. "The Secret Service is not altogether happy about your background, you know."

"Who would be?"

I laughed. She didn't.

"I'm afraid you'll have to get used to men in dark suits, Jenny. They're in your future. And chances are good that, sooner, later, your story will get out."

"I knew that when I contacted you."

"I'm sure you did. So all these years you've kept the lowest possible profile, doing everything you could to stay off the radar, and now you're willing to give it all up. Why?"

"I don't have the slightest idea," I said.

Late that night I lay still awake in bed remembering, of all things, how Michael, that first time, had so lovingly overlooked my scars.

14

SATURDAY'S RAIN, as it turned out, was only a harbinger. Briefly the skies cleared, then came a storm that flooded low-lying streets and took out power in a full third of the city. Cars slid sideways into culverts, patio furniture was swept like spawning salmon toward the sea, water and mud came up under the doors of downtown shops. Standing inside the glass doors of the studio, we saw a cat in a garbage-can lid, paw lifted as though in greeting or entreaty as it spun past, down the middle of Connecticut Avenue. Lightning threw itself against the sky again and again, tossing our faces from sudden, ghostly light to near dark there behind those heavy doors. Never before had I noticed how much lightning resembled something human—our circulatory system, or the many branches and sub-branches of trachea, bronchi, bronchioles.

I really *didn't* have the slightest idea, and that bothered me. Logic and common sense were the cornerposts of my life, stars I steered by. Whatever problems emerged, I liked to think, I could assess them coolly, decide how they could best be resolved, take action to that end. But now I found myself sailing boldly out, and with no map. Why was I willing to endanger this life I'd so carefully sculpted for myself, only to bring scarce comfort to a woman I hardly knew?

Question the motives, Mickie always said, *especially those of altruists.*

"Impressive," she said now as we stood watching the storm. "Even in a town so accustomed to shows of power."

I'd passed the morning fulfilling my function as Waring blender. Chunks of videotape, feeds from the networks, odd bits of documentation, and the occasional still photo get thrown at me, and I snicker-snack them down to a palatable paste. The rough cut goes to Mickie, who while *she* watches is thinking about getting the whole story told, contrast, balance, and flow, possible voice-overs or superimpositions; then it comes back to me with her notes, from which I remix. We've worked together a long time, like to think we're off the block before other runners ever realize the gun's been fired.

"The cut's okay?" I asked.

"Luis's cleaning and framing as we speak."

"It's thin."

"So is the air we're breathing right now. Got a minute, Jenny?"

We turned from the glass doors outside of which the world was dissolving and its remains being washed away, back into the studio, to her office. Things she insisted on calling tikis hung thick on every wall: a couple of primitive masks from a trip to Tahiti, gold-rimmed souvenir plates bearing likenesses of JFK and Martin Luther King, a pair of roller skates in a shadow box, paper tole icons of butterflies, birds and a beach scene painstakingly crafted, layer upon layer, by her mother, set in plastic frames grained to look like wood.

Mickie sat, waited till I did the same, looked off at one of the windows, then back at me. "You should know that word is getting out, Jenny. A slow leak for the moment. But."

"It's not the leak, it's the pressure behind it."

Mickie nodded.

"From somewhere in the Secret Service?"

"Presumably. An assistant, a secretary or scheduler . . ." Rain slammed against the window. Mickie glanced that way again. "Be careful, Jenny. Lot of people out there'd want to use you to their advantage."

"We're talking about the president."

"Yes."

"But you know the rest, don't you?"

"Of course I do."

"All these years, you never once said anything."

"It's your life, Jenny. Others have a right only to those portions of it you offer."

Odd sentiments from a newswoman. Neither of us spoke for a while. Finally I thanked her and said that I should get back to work.

Power was shut down in the lobby where we'd stood watching and in nonessential parts of the studio, but emergency generators served the rest. Back in my safe haven, I sat for a long time lost, window behind me streaming with rain, screens before me streaming with images. Not much difference in the two.

That night I sloshed my way over to the neighbors, to see how Snake and his squatter band had fared with the storms. Even as I approached, I somehow knew. Then I saw the plastic garbage bags lined up at curbside.

They were gone. They had put the house in order, left the

place just as they found it, put all their discards, everything they weren't taking with them, in the bags out front.

On the kitchen table was a note.

TIME TO MOVE ON
THANKS FOR EVERYTHING JENNY

On the back, they'd made a list of everything—all just *things*—I'd given them, the food, the blankets and sheets, the utensils and dishes and tableware, patent medicines. No way I could know, but from the variety of handwriting I had the notion that every one of them had a part in the note. I imagined them standing around the table, Snake or Josie or Buddy jotting down a few words, looking up to say Your turn.

15

JUST OVER A MONTH LATER, Grace handed me a mug of coffee as I rushed past (think trains and mail bags and you've an apposite image) and said, "Please tell the president how sorry we are, and that we're praying for her."

So the cat wasn't just out of the bag, it was sitting on the wall in bright sunlight for all to see.

"I will, Grace. I definitely will. How's Jeb?"

"He passed last night. Peacefully, in his sleep."

"At the hospital?"

She nodded.

The collar of her blouse was hiked up in the back. I reached to set it straight, and when I did, for just a moment, I thought she was going to pull away.

"I'm so sorry. Why are you even here?"

"Because I need to be."

She saw what I was about to protest: that, yes, news was breaking and, yes, we all depended shamefully upon her, but.

"I need to be here for *me*, Jenny."

"I understand." Better than most, I suspect. It's work that's saved me and goes on doing so.

"Oh," Grace said, handing me a slip, "this woman's been calling."

Edith Smith. Mrs. Horace Smith.

Back in the studio, where I rarely used the phone, I dialed.

"Thank you for calling back," she said.

"I just now got your messages."

"When you came to see us . . ." She grew silent. I waited. "I knew why you were here. Who you were."

"Yes. I thought you might."

"I'm so sorry. It was more than I could take on. I had my hands full just taking care of Horace. Those last months, he faded in and out, he'd be there one moment, be missing the next. I mean, he was *there*, but. . . ."

"I understand."

"Many's the time I'd walk in and find him weeping over a TV commercial. One day a bird started building its nest on a ledge outside one of the windows and he stood there for hours watching, tears streaming down his face. He'd become so emotional, and after every outbreak he was ill for days. How could he possibly handle the appearance in his life of a lost daughter?"

"Why did you call, Mrs. Smith?"

"He's gone. My Horace is gone. A stroke, they say. We never know, they tell me, with time he may come back, we'll just have to wait and see, we don't know. But I look into his eyes and *I* know."

"I'm sorry for you, Mrs. Smith. And for your husband. I'm still not fixed on why you're calling."

"I'm all alone, Miss Rowan. You don't have to be my daughter, I've no right to ask that. But I need a friend just now."

Friend seemed to be the role I was meant to take. Cheryl.

Mickie. The president, for God's sake. Now my own mother—a total stranger.

"Are you at home?"

"Yes."

"I'll be right there."

I was with my father when the bomb, missile, whatever—for a long time we didn't know, but it was an RPG, a rocket-propelled grenade—struck the White House. Edith stood behind me as I held his hand. She and I had turned to watch it happen again on the TV mounted high on the wall, and when we turned back, his eyes were open.

"I'm sorry, I can't remember your name, young lady," he said.

"Jenny. It's Jenny."

"Of course. All you nurses are very kind here." His eyes went to the TV. Another clip of the breached west wing, smoke and fire everywhere. "You seen that?"

"Yes, sir, I have."

"What's this country come to?" He watched a while. "Terrible, just terrible. None of us are safe. You be careful out there, you hear me, Jenny?"

"Yes, sir."

Then he smiled, patted my hand, and died.

I stayed with Edith well into the afternoon. From time to time, those first hours, I clicked on the TV or radio hoping to learn more, but no one had got it sorted and all we had was your essential tape loop, the same niggardly bits of information going round and round in a stutter.

Sarah was all right, though. When the rocket struck, she'd been on the hill conferring with congressional leaders.

"Isn't it protocol," CBS anchor Bill Whiting said, hair and necktie perfect, ever-present sparkle in his eyes, "that congressmen come to the president, not the other way round?"

"Ordinarily, yes," his expert guest said. I remembered Mickie's jest that Whiting's sparkle had been surgically implanted. "Tradition more than protocol, perhaps. But"—he paused meaningfully and tugged at his own tie, perhaps hoping it might come to look as good as Bill's—"this is not a president who does things in the usual manner."

"Definitely not." And here was Bill squinting to read the scroll on the prompter. Scuttlebutt had it that the network had offered to buy him contacts but he was afraid they'd dim the sparkle. "Employment has taken a dramatic upward swing. The economy as a whole, in fact. And as the song says, she's only just begun."

Meanwhile, I thought, the whole country had gone amnesiac, forgetting that Sarah's son had been abducted and remained missing. Amazing what a loud bang in the sky overhead and prospects of an improved GNP can obscure. In a sense, of course, she'd stopped being Sarah. She'd become an icon, an image, a symbol. Agendas and propagandas, the loss and longing of a whole population, were busily attaching themselves to her like barnacles.

I was preparing to take leave of Edith, one more pot of tea and I'd be gone, when the buzzer sounded.

I answered the door, and one of the suit people stood there.

"Miss Rowan," he said.

"Good God."

"Not quite." Behind him, at curbside, car doors opened and

Sarah emerged. She came up the four stairs of the porch and held out her hand.

"I heard about your father. I'm so sorry."

Not a sign of media anywhere.

I showed her in and introduced her to Edith. Sarah said she was sorry to hear about her husband and offered condolences.

"Condolences don't mean much, I know, given the magnitude of your loss. If there's anything . . ."

Edith, stoic until that moment, burst into tears.

Our president settled beside her on the sofa, saying that she couldn't stay long.

16

A FEATURE PIECE in the *Washington Post* got picked up by the wire services and the Internet. Mickie phoned at five A.M. to warn me. Pure American Dream stuff, spun cotton candy. Much-abused woman pulls herself by her bootstraps right smack out of the horrors of her past to become a productive citizen, a creative force really, and—where else but in America?—befriends the president in *her* hour of need.

Wow. And hand me a tissue.

The amnesia seemed to be passing, at least, and that was a good thing: the country had been reminded what befell Sarah and son.

I'd always understood that America is as much idea as actuality, a focused amnesia instrumental to that idea's power. Women forget the pain of childbirth, body and mind file away trauma where it can't be accessed, the state with its grand ideals must look away from whatever belies those ideals. Henry James claimed that in America each new generation is a new people. Each day here is also a new day, unburdened by history, rife with promise.

"Don't suppose I should come in, then," I had said when Mickie called.

"What, with us just starting to get reports and footage on the White House strike? And we're supposed to handle all this without our top editor? You damn well better come in."

"You've got other editors."

"What I've got is people who, if they hadn't gone to goddamn trade school, would be stocking supermarket shelves, working part-time at Walmart for no benefits."

"You drive a hard bargain."

"That's why I'm still around, sweetie. You have any idea how many I've seen just fade away?"

"I'll be in by eight, latest."

I soaked in a bath as I drank half a pot of coffee, read half an Ed McBain novel, and knocked back two pieces of grilled flatbread. Before I left, I looked in on Cheryl, still dead asleep. I was fairly sure she had an early class today, but hey, it was her life.

Close to nine, I parked in the alley behind the studio and ducked into the service entrance. By noon I had a rough cut of the White House attack. Remembering *Dr. Strangelove*, I'd assembled it as a kind of ballet: explosion like the bloom of a huge white flower, draw back to the faces of standersby, then clouds above and an untroubled sky, comments of interviewees folded in as leitmotifs, citizens of DC going about their business, Sarah looking through papers aboard Air Force One, firemen's faces streaming with sweat, children at play in the park, the explosion again. Somehow I'd managed to build a three-four beat into the whole thing. Ravel, whose *La Valse* well could serve as the sound track of our time, would have been proud.

"This'll do just fine," Mickie said, "as it is."

"But it's only a rough cut."

"Which is why it works so well. The ragged edges show. The

rawness. It's exactly what's going on in all our minds—images, confusion, a jumble of words we can't absorb and feelings we can't voice, this sense of a world gone suddenly sideways."

She picked up her phone.

"Marc? Where are we on the clock? What, five or six minutes in? Kill it. Cut in, announce an exclusive special feature. I'm shooting it up to you now. Run it whole, no interruptions—and no, I don't give a damn what the schedule says."

She hung up.

"The call's yours, Jenny. I can keep the credits off this. You know as well as I do, once your name scrolls up, they'll be on it like jackals."

"I don't need credit."

"They may get onto it anyway."

"Then at least we'll know we made them work for it."

Mickie smiled. "Attitude's everything." Snaring my letter of resignation, which I'd brought her along with the tape, she held it up. "This what you really want?"

"Do you see an alternative?"

For a moment, as our eyes held, there was nothing else in the world.

"From your perspective, no," she said finally. "But I'd as soon hack off both arms as lose you. Where will you go?"

"I don't know."

Mickie nodded. "I hope you'll be in touch, once you settle. Let me know you're okay, if nothing else."

"I'll always be okay."

Standing, Mickie held out her hand, and we shook. "It's all just one box after another, Jenny."

· · ·

I'd promised to meet Edith for lunch. As I went out past her desk, Grace said, "You may not want your call slips."

"No way." The sheaf she held out had the thickness of a desk-top calendar.

I was almost through the door before I turned back. "You have plans for lunch, Grace?"

"Usually I just bring in a salad, can of tuna and crackers, something like that, eat here at the desk."

"Any interest in taking a walk on the wild side? I'm meeting my mother for lunch. You could join us."

She did, and the two of them hit it off instantly. Three months later, they'd move in together. They lived together for six years till Edith died, leaving the house to Grace, who's still there.

I heard all this from Cheryl, who'd taken over my apartment, now rapidly filling with children whose photos hang on my refrigerator. Joanie, an adorable curly-headed blond of five. Katie, almost exactly a year younger, dark hair, serious demeanor. Baby Kyle looking faintly demonic in his crib. Cheryl's husband Carl sounds a marvel. By profession a small-animal veterinarian, he's a lay preacher in his church. Many an evening, sitting at the kitchen table here in my apartment in Miami at the edge of the known world, just as I used to sit at my red-and-white table in the old place, Cheryl's place now, I think how much I'd like to meet Carl. But I live in a different world these days, and largely in Spanish.

Ten thirty. My shift begins in half an hour. How many shootings and knifings, how many incontrovertible accidents, will grace our ER tonight? How many IVs will I start, how many endotracheal tubes hand to the doctor on duty? How many hands old and young will I hold even as I feel them go lax and empty in my own?

17

A WEEK AFTER I LEFT, just past dawn, they found Reagan's body. A rookie patrol officer on a slow crawl through an alley noticed a concentration of rats around a fifty-gallon drum theretofore used by street people for fires and pulled up, car door open, motor left running, stopped to look in.

I watched the news from my new apartment at world's edge. Jack Collins stood looking tired and gorgeous behind a podium honeycombed with microphones. There's no way adequately to express how much I longed in my heart to reach out to Sarah then. She in turn had resources that could have found me easily enough. But like Mickie she respected my choice. Cheryl is the only one I keep in touch with.

Heath bars and Magic 8-Balls, squatter Josie's limp-doll baby, Jack's warmth beside me in bed—memory will cut you off at the knees if you let it.

Speaking of the Magic 8-Ball, I just now gave it two turns.

Outlook good.

Don't count on it.

I should tell you that everything above was written months

ago in a burst, most of it in two days and the night between, fueled by infusions of coffee and dark beer, before I stalled out with no idea how to end.

In the interim Sarah Courtney-Phillips nears the end of her elected full term with an unprecedented 72 percent approval rate. Like Jack, she looks good on TV these days. Well appointed, well groomed, eyebrows shaved and redrawn, a new haircut. Her daughter is often beside her.

I still have no idea how to finish. I'm supposed to tie it all up, I know, supposed to bring to light structures not easily evident, set the whole to a low boil as it were, reduce by half, add salt of irony, pepper of erudition, herbs and spices to taste.

But there's really no structure here—only my life.

So here's the only ending I have.

I remember how it felt when the box was pulled out. I'd hear the footsteps first. Then the jolt along my spine as we, the box and I, slid. And the miraculous opening. More than anything, I think, I would hope to have you feel that moment in all its wonder and surprise. I know you can't understand. What an amazing gift it was when the box was opened.

I wish you all good openings, and wonder, and surprise.

A NOTE ON THE AUTHOR

James Sallis is the acclaimed author of more than two dozen volumes of fiction, poetry, translation, essays, and criticism, including the Lew Griffin cycle, *Drive, Cypress Grove, Cripple Creek, The Killer Is Dying,* and *Salt River.* His biography of the great crime writer Chester Himes is an acknowledged classic. Sallis lives in Phoenix, Arizona, with his wife, Karyn.